THE SCALEHUNTER'S BEAUTIFUL DAUGHTER

THE SCALEHUNTER'S BEAUTIFUL DAUGHTER

LUCIUS SHEPARD

THE SCALEHUNTER'S BEAUTIFUL DAUGHTER

published by
Mark V. Ziesing
Post Office Box 806
Willimantic, CT 06226

The publisher wishes to thank Andy Watson
for helping to produce this book.

FIRST EDITION

Signed Edition ISBN 0-9612970-9-3
Trade Edition ISBN 0-9612970-8-5
LC No. 87-051693

For Bob, Karol, and Timalyne Frazier

One

Not long after the Christlight of the world's first morning faded, when birds still flew to heaven and back, and even the wickedest things shone like saints, so pure was their portion of evil, there was a village by the name of Hangtown that clung to the back of the dragon Griaule, a vast mile-long beast who had been struck immobile yet not lifeless by a wizard's spell, and who ruled over the Carbonales Valley, controlling in every detail the lives of the inhabitants, making known his will by the ineffable radiations emanating from the cold tonnage of his brain. From shoulder to tail, the greater part of Griaule was covered with earth and trees and grass, from some perspectives appearing to be an element of the landscape, another

hill among those that ringed the valley;
except for sections cleared by the scalehunters, only a portion of his right side to
the haunch, and his massive neck and
head remained visible, and the head had
sunk to the ground, its massive jaws
halfway open, itself nearly as high as the
crests of the surrounding hills. Situated
almost eight hundred feet above the valley
floor and directly behind the fronto-
parietal plate, which overhung the place
like a mossy cliff, the village consisted of
several dozen shacks with shingled roofs
and walls of weathered planking, and
bordered a lake fed by a stream that ran
down onto Griaule's back from an
adjoining hill; it was hemmed in against
the shore by thickets of chokecherry,
stands of stunted oak and hawthornes,
and but for the haunted feeling that
pervaded the air, a vibrant stillness similar
to the atmosphere of an old ruin, to
someone standing beside the lake it would
seem he was looking out upon an ordinary
country settlement, one a touch less neatly
ordered than most, littered as it was with
the bones and entrails of skizzers and
flakes and other parasites that infested the
dragon, but nonetheless ordinary in the

lassitide that governed it, and the shabby dress and hostile attitudes of its citizenry.

Many of the inhabitants of the village were scalehunters, men and women who scavenged under Griaule's earth-encrusted wings and elsewhere on his body, searching for scales that were cracked and broken, chipping off fragments and selling these in Port Chantay, where they were valued for their medicinal properties. They were well paid for their efforts, but were treated as pariahs by the people of the valley, who rarely ventured onto the dragon, and their lives were short and fraught with unhappy incident, a circumstance they attributed to the effects of Griaule's displeasure at their presence. Indeed, his displeasure was a constant preoccupation, and they spent much of their earnings on charms that they believed would ward off its evil influence. Some wore bits of scale around their necks, hoping that this homage would communicate to Griaule the high regard in which they held him, and perhaps the most extreme incidence of this way of thinking was embodied by the nurture given by the widower Riall to his daughter Catherine. On the day of her birth, also the day of his wife's death, he dug down beneath the floor of his shack until he reached Griaule's back, laying bare a patch of golden scale some six feet long and five feet wide, and from that day forth for the next eighteen years he forced her to sleep upon the scale, hoping that the dragon's essence would seep into her and so she would be protected against his wrath. Catherine complained at first about this isolation, but she came to enjoy the dreams that visited her, dreams of flying, of otherworldly climes (according to legend, dragons were native to another universe to which they traveled by flying into the sun); lying there sometimes, looking up through the plank-shored tunnel her father had dug, she would feel that she was not resting on a solid surface but was receding from the earth, falling into a golden distance.

Riall may or may not have achieved his desired end; but it was evident to the people of Hangtown that propinquity to the scale had left its mark on Catherine, for while Riall was short and swarthy (as his wife had also been), physically unprepossessing in every respect, his daughter had grown into a beautiful young woman,

long-limbed and slim, with fine golden hair
and and lovely skin and a face of
unsurpassed delicacy, seeming a lapidary
creation with its voluptuous mouth and
sharp cheekbones and large, eloquent
eyes, whose irises were so dark that they
could be distinguished from the pupils
only under the strongest of lights. Not
alone in her beauty did she appear cut
from different cloth from her parents;
neither did she share their gloomy spirit
and cautious approach to life. From
earliest childhood she went without fear to
every quarter of the dragon's surface, even
into the darkness under the wing joints
where few scalehunters dared go; she
believed she had been immunized against
ordinary dangers by her father's tactics,
and she felt there was a bond between
herself and the dragon, that her dreams
and good looks were emblems of both a
magical relationship and consequential
destiny, and this feeling of invulnerability
— along with the confidence instilled by
her beauty — gave rise to a certain
egocentricity and shallowness of character. She was often disdainful, careless in
the handling of lovers' hearts, and though
she did not stoop to duplicity — she had

no need of that — she took pleasure in stealing the men whom other women loved. And yet she considered herself a good woman. Not a saint, mind you. But she honored her father and kept the house clean and did her share of work, and though she had her faults, she had taken steps — half-steps, rather — to correct them. Like most people, she had no clear moral determinant, depending upon taboos and specific circumstances to modify her behavior, and the "good," the principled, was to her a kind of intellectual afterlife to which she planned some day to aspire, but only after she had exhausted the potentials of pleasure and thus gained the experience necessary for the achievement of such an aspiration. She was prone to bouts of moodiness, as were all within the sphere of Griaule's influence, but generally displayed a sunny disposition and optimistic cast of thought. This is not to say, however, that she was a Pollyanna, an innocent. Through her life in Hangtown she was familiar with treachery, grief, and murder, and at eighteen she had already been with a wide variety of lovers. Her easy sexuality was typical of Hangtown's populace, yet because of her beauty and the jealousy it had engendered, she had acquired the reputation of being exceptionally wanton. She was amused, even somewhat pleased, by her reputation, but the rumors surrounding her grew more scurrilous, more deviant from the truth, and eventually there came a day when they were brought home to her with a savagery that she could never have presupposed.

Beyond Griaule's frontal spike, which rose from a point between his eyes, a great whorled horn curving back toward Hangtown, the slope of the skull flattened out into the top of his snout, and it was here that Catherine came one foggy morning, dressed in loose trousers and a tunic, equipped with scaling hooks and ropes and chisels, intending to chip off a sizeable piece of cracked scale she had noticed near the dragon's lip, a spot directly above one of the fangs. She worked at the piece for several hours, suspended by linkages of rope over Griaule's lower jaw. His half-open mouth was filled with a garden of evil-looking plants, the calloused surface of his forked tongue showing here and there between the leaves like nodes of red coral; his fangs were inscribed with intricate patterns of lichen, wreathed by streamers of fog and circled by raptors who now and then would plummet into the bushes to skewer some unfortunate lizard or vole. Epiphytes bloomed from splits in the ivory, depending long strings of interwoven red and purple blossoms. It was a compelling sight, and from time to time Catherine would stop working and lower herself in her harness until she was no more than fifty feet above the tops of the bushes and look off into the caliginous depths of Griaule's throat, wondering at the nature of the shadowy creatures that flitted there.

The sun burned off the fog, and Catherine, sweaty, weary of chipping, hauled herself up to the top of the snout and stretched out on the scales, resting on an elbow, nibbling at a honey pear and gazing out over the valley with its spiny green hills and hammocks of thistle palms and the faraway white buildings of Teocinte, where that very night she planned to dance and make love. The air became so warm that she stripped off her tunic and lay back, bare to the waist, eyes closed, daydreaming in the clean spring-time heat. She had been drifting between sleep and waking for the better part of an hour, when a scraping noise brought her alert. She reached for her tunic and started to sit up; but before she could turn to see who or what had made the sound, something fell heavily across her ribs, taking her wind, leaving her gasping and disoriented. A hand groped her breast, and she smelled winey breath.

"Go easy, now," said a man's voice, thickened with urgency. "I don't want nothing half of Hangtown ain't had already."

Catherine twisted her head, and caught a glimpse of Key Willen's lean, sallow face looming above her, his sardonic mouth hitched at one corner in a half-smile.

"I told you we'd have our time," he said, fumbling with the tie of her trousers.

She began to fight desperately, clawing at his eyes, catching a handful of his long black hair and yanking. She threw herself onto her stomach, clutching at the edge of a scale, trying to worm out from beneath him; but he butted her in the temple, sending white lights shooting through her skull. Once her head had cleared, she found that he had flipped her onto her back, had pulled her trousers down past her hips and penetrated her with his fingers; he was working them in and out, his breath coming hoarse and rapid. She felt raw inside, and she let out a sharp, throat-tearing scream. She thrashed about, tearing at his shirt, his hair, screaming again and again, and when he clamped his free hand to her mouth, she bit it.

"You bitch! You . . . goddamn . . . " He slammed the back of her head against the scale, climbed atop her, straddling her chest and pinning her shoulders with his knees. He slapped her, wrapped his hand in her hair, and leaned close, spittle flying to her face as he spoke. "You listen up, pig! I don't much care if you're awake . . . One way or the other, I'm gonna have my fun." He rammed her head into the scale again. "You hear me? Hear me?" He straightened, slapped her harder. "Hell, I'm having fun right now."

"Please!" she said, dazed.

"'Please?'" He laughed. "That mean you want some more?" Another slap. "You like it?"

Yet another slap.

"How 'bout that?"

Frantic, she wrenched an arm free, in reflex reaching up behind her head, searching for a weapon, anything, and as he prepared to slap her again, grinning, she caught hold of a stick — or so she thought — and swung it at him in a vicious arc. The point of the scaling hook, for such it was, sank into Key's flesh just back of his left eye, and as he fell, toppling sideways with only the briefest of outcries, the eye filled with blood, becoming a featureless crimson sphere like a rubber ball embedded in the socket. Catherine shrieked, pushed his legs off her waist and scrambled away, encumbered by her trousers, which had slipped down about her knees. Key's body convulsed, his heels drumming the scale. She sat staring at him for a long seamless time, unable to catch her breath, to think. But swarms of black flies, their translucent wings shattering the sunlight into prism, began landing on the puddle of blood that spread wide as a table from beneath Key's face, and she became queasy. She crawled to the edge of the snout and looked away across the checkerboard of fields below toward Port Chantay, toward an alp of bubbling cumulus building from the horizon. Her chest hollowed with cold, and she started to shake. The tremors passing through her echoed the tremor she had felt in Key's body when the hook had bit into his skull. All the sickness inside her, her shock and disgust at the violation, at confronting the substance of death, welled up in her throat and her stomach emptied. When she had finished she cinched her trousers tight, her fingers clumsy with the knot. She thought she should do something. Coil the ropes, maybe. Store the harness in her pack. But these actions, while easy to contemplate, seemed impossibly complex to carry out. She shivered and hugged herself, feeling the altitude, the distances. Her cheeks were feverish and puffy; flickers of sensation — she pictured them to be irridescent worms — tingled nerves in her chest and legs. She had the idea that everything was slowing, that time had flurried and was settling the way river mud settles after the passage of some turbulence. She stared off toward the dragon's horn. Someone was standing there. Coming toward her, now. At first she watched the figure approach with a defiant disinterest, wanting to guard her privacy, feeling that if she had to speak she would lose control of her emotions. But as the figure resolved into one of her neighbors back in

Hangtown — Brianne, a tall young woman with brittle good looks, dark brown hair and an olive complexion — she relaxed from this attitude. She and Brianne were not friends; in fact, they had once been rivals for the same man. However, that had been a year and more in the past, and Catherine was relieved to see her. More than relieved. The presence of another woman allowed her to surrender to weakness, believing that in Brianne she would find a fund of natural sympathy because of their common sex.

"My God, what happened?" Brianne kneeled and brushed Catherine's hair back from her eyes. The tenderness of the gesture burst the damn of Catherine's emotions, and punctuating the story with sobs, she told of the rape.

"I didn't mean to kill him," she said. "I . . . I'd forgotten about the hook."

"Key was looking to get killed," Brianne said. "But it's a damn shame you had to be the one to help him along." She sighed, her forehead creased by a worry line. "I suppose I should fetch someone to take care of the body. I know that's not . . . "

"No, I understand . . . it has to be done." Catherine felt stronger, more capable. She made as if to stand, but Brianne restrained her.

"Maybe you should wait here. You know how people will be. They'll see your face," — she touched Catherine's swollen cheeks — "and they'll be prying, whispering. It might be better to let the mayor come out and make his investigation. That way he can take the edge off the gossip before it gets started."

Catherine didn't want to be alone with the body any longer, but she saw the wisdom in waiting and agreed.

"Will you be all right?" Brianne asked.

"I'll be fine . . . but hurry."

"I will." Brianne stood; the wind feathered her hair, lifted it to veil the lower half of her face. "You're sure you'll be all right?" There was an odd undertone in her voice, as if it were really another question she was asking, or — and this, Catherine thought, was more likely — as if she were thinking ahead to dealing with the mayor.

Catherine nodded, then caught at Brianne as she started to walk away. "Don't tell my father. Let me tell him. If he hears it from you, he might go after the Willens."

"I won't say a thing, I promise."

With a smile, a sympathetic pat on the arm, Brianne headed back toward Hangtown, vanishing into the thickets that sprang up beyond the frontal spike. For awhile after she had gone, Catherine felt wrapped in her consolation; but the seething of the wind, the chill that infused the air as clouds moved in to cover the sun, these things caused the solitude of the place and the grimness of the circumstance to close down around her, and she began to wish she had returned to Hangtown. She squeezed her eyes shut, trying to steady herself, but even then she kept seeing Key's face, his bloody eye, and remembering his hands on her. Finally, thinking that Brianne had had more than enough time to accomplish her task, she walked up past the frontal spike and stood looking out along the narrow trail that wound through the thickets on Griaule's back. Several minutes elapsed, and then she spotted three figures — two men and a woman — coming at a brisk pace. She shaded her eyes against a ray of sun that had broken through the overcast, and peered at them. Neither man had the gray hair and portly shape of Hangtown's mayor. They were lanky, pale, with black hair falling to their shoulders, and were carrying unsheathed knives. Catherine couldn't make out their faces, but she realized that Brianne must not have set aside their old rivalry, that in the spirit of vengeance she had informed Key's brothers of his death.

Fear cut through the fog of shock, and she tried to think what to do. There was only the one trail and no hope that she could hide in the thickets. She retreated toward the edge of the snout, stepping around the patch of drying blood. Her only chance for escape would be to lower herself on the ropes and take refuge in Griaule's mouth; however, the thought of entering so ominous a place, a place shunned by all but the mad, gave her pause. She tried to think of alternatives, but there were none. Brianne would no doubt have lied to the Willens, cast her as the guilty party, and the brothers would never listen to her. She hurried to the edge, buckled on the harness and slipped over the side, working with frenzied speed, lowering in ten and fifteen foot drops. Her view of the mouth lurched and veered — a panorama of bristling leaves and head-high ferns, enormous fangs hooking up from the jaw and pitch-dark emptiness at the entrance to the throat. She was fifty feet from the surface when she felt the rope jerking, quivering; glancing up, she saw that one of the Willens was sawing at it with his knife. Her heart felt hot and throbbing in her chest, her palms were slick. She dropped half the distance to the jaw, stopping with a jolt that sent pain shooting through her spine and left her swinging back and forth, muddle-headed. She began another drop, a shorter one, but the rope parted high above and she fell the last twenty feet, landing with such stunning force that she lost consciousness.

She came to in a bed of ferns, staring up through the fronds at the dull brick-colored roof of Griaule's mouth, a surface festooned with spiky dark green epiphytes, like the vault of a cathedral that had been invaded by the jungle. She lay still for a moment, gathering herself, testing the aches that mapped her body to determine if anything was broken. A lump sprouted from the back of the head, but the brunt of the impact had been absorbed by her rear end, and though she felt pain there, she didn't think the damage was severe. Moving cautiously, wincing, she came to

her knees and was about to stand when
she heard shouts from above.

"See her?"

"Naw ... you?"

"She musta gone deeper in!"

Catherine peeked between the fronds
and saw two dark figures centering
networks of ropes, suspended a hundred
feet or so overhead like spiders with
simple webs. They dropped lower, and
panicked, she crawled on her belly away
from the mouth, hauling herself along by
gripping twists of dead vine that formed a
matte underlying the foliage. After she
had gone about fifty yards she looked
back. The Willens were hanging barely a
dozen feet above the tops of the bushes,
and as she watched they lowered out of
sight. Her instincts told her to move
deeper into the mouth, but the air was
considerably darker where she now
kneeled than where she had landed — a
grayish green gloom — and the idea of
penetrating the greater darkness of
Griaule's throat stalled her heart. She
listened for the Willens and heard
slitherings, skitterings, and rustles. Eerie
whistles that, although soft, were complex
and articulated. She imagined that these

were not the cries of tiny creatures but the
gutterings of breath in a huge throat, and
she had a terrifying sense of the size of the
place, of her own relative insignificance.
She couldn't bring herself to continue in
deeper, and she made her way toward the
side of the mouth, where thick growths of
ferns flourished in the shadow. When she
reached a spot at which the mouth sloped
upward, she buried herself among the
ferns and kept very still.

Next to her head was an irregular
patch of pale red flesh, where a clump of
soil had been pulled away by an uprooted
plant. Curious, she extended a forefinger
and found it cool and dry. It was like
touching stone or wood, and that
disappointed her; she had, she realized,
been hoping the touch would affect her in
some extreme way. She pressed her palm
to the flesh, trying to detect the tic of a
pulse, but the flesh was inert, and the
rustlings and the occasional beating of
wings overhead were the only signs of life.
She began to grow drowsy, to nod, and
she fought to keep awake. But after a few
minutes she let herself relax. The more
she examined the situation, the more
convinced she became that the Willens

would not track her this far; the extent of
their nerve would be to wait at the verge
of the mouth, to lay siege to her, knowing
that eventually she would have to seek
food and water. Thinking about water
made her thirsty, but she denied the
craving. She needed rest far more. And
removing one of the scaling hooks from
her belt, holding it in her right hand in case
some animal less cautious than the
Willens happened by, she pillowed her
head against the pale red patch of
Griaule's flesh and was soon fast asleep.

Two

Many of Catherine's dreams over the years had seemed sendings rather than distillations of experience, but never had she had one so clearly of that character as the dream she had that afternoon in Griaule's mouth. It was a simple dream, formless, merely a voice whose words less came to her ear than enveloped her, steeping her in their meanings, and of them she retained only a message of reassurance, of security, one so profound that it instilled in her a confidence that lasted even after she waked into a world gone black, the sole illumination being the gleams of reflected firelight that flowed along the curve of one of the fangs. It was an uncanny sight, that huge tooth glazed with fierce red shine, and under other circumstances she would have been frightened by it; but in this instance she did not react to the barbarity of the image and saw it instead as evidence that her suppositions concerning the Willens had been correct. They had built a fire near the lip and were watching for her, expecting her to bolt into their arms. But she had no intention of fulfilling their expectations. Although her confidence flickered on and off, although to go deeper into the dragon seemed irrational, she knew that any other course offered the certainty of a knife stroke across the neck. And, too, despite the apparent rationality of her decision, she had an unshakable feeling that Griaule was watching over her, that his will was being effected. She had a flash vision of Key Willen's face, his gaping mouth and blood-red eye, and recalled her terror at his assault. However, these memories no longer harrowed her. They steadied her, resolving certain questions that — while she had never asked them — had always been there to ask. She hadn't been to blame in any way for the rape, she had not tempted Key. But she saw that she had left herself open to tragedy by her aimlessness, by her reliance on a vague sense of destiny to give life meaning. Now it appeared that her destiny was at hand, and she understood that its violent coloration might have been different had *she* been different, had she engaged the world with energy and not with a passive attitude. She hoped that knowing all this would prove important, but she doubted that it would, believing that she had gone too far on the wrong path for any degree of knowledge to matter.

It took all her self-control to begin her journey inward, feeling her way along the side of the throat, pushing through ferns and cobwebs, her hands encountering unfamiliar textures that made her skin crawl, alert to the burbling of insects and other night creatures. On one occasion she was close to turning back, but she heard shouts behind her, and fearful that the Willens were on her trail, she kept going. As she started down an incline, she saw a faint gleam riding the curve of the throat wall. The glow brightened, casting the foliage into silhouette, and eager to reach the source, she picked up her pace, tripping over roots, vines snagging her ankles. At length the incline flattened out, and she emerged into a large chamber,

roughly circular in shape, its upper regions
lost in darkness; upon the floor lay pools
of black liquid; mist trailed across the
surface of the pools, and whenever the
mist lowered to touch the liquid, a fringe
of yellowish red flame would flare up,
cutting the shadows on the pebbled skin
of the floor and bringing to light a number
of warty knee-high protuberances that
sprouted among the pools — these were
deep red in color, perforated around the
sides, leaking pale threads of mist. At the
rear of the chamber was an opening that
Catherine assumed led farther into the
dragon. The air was warm, dank, and a
sweat broke out all over her body. She
balked at entering the chamber; in spite of
the illumination, it was a less human place
than the mouth. But once again she
forced herself onward, stepping carefully
between the fires and, after discovering
that the mist made her giddy, giving the
protuberances a wide berth. Piercing
whistles came from above. The notion
that this might signal the presence of bats
caused her to hurry, and she had covered
half the distance across when a man's
voice called to her, electrifying her with
fear.

"Catherine!" he said. "Not so fast!"

She spun about, her scaling hook at the ready. Hobbling toward her was an elderly white-haired man dressed in the ruin of a silk frock coat embroidered with gold thread, a tattered ruffled shirt, and holed satin leggings. In his left hand he carried a gold-knobbed cane, and at least a dozen glittering rings encircled his bony fingers. He stopped an arm's length away, leaning on his cane, and although Catherine did not lower her hook, her fear diminished. Despite the eccentricity of his appearance, considering the wide spectrum of men and creatures who inhabited Griaule, he seemed comparatively ordinary, a reason for caution but not alarm.

"Ordinary?" The old man cackled. "Oh yes, indeed! Ordinary as angels, as unexceptional as the idea of God!" Before she had a chance to wonder at his knowledge of her thoughts, he let out another cackle. "How could I not know them? We are every one of us creatures of his thought, expressions of his whim. And here what is only marginally evident on the surface becomes vivid reality, inescapable truth. For here," — he poked the chamber floor with his cane — "here we live in the medium of his will." He hobbled a step closer, fixing her with a rheumy stare. "I have dreamed this moment a thousand times. I know what you will say, what you will think, what you will do. He has instructed me in all your particulars so that I may become your guide, your confidant."

"What are you talking about?" Catherine hefted her hook, her anxiety increasing.

"Not 'what'," said the old man. "Who." A grin split the pale wrinkled leather of his face. "His Scaliness, of course."

"Griaule?"

"None other." The old man held out his hand. "Come along now, girl. They're waiting for us."

Catherine drew back.

The old man pursed his lips. "Well, I suppose you could return the way you came. The Willens will be happy to see you."

Flustered, Catherine said, "I don't understand. How can you know . . . "

"Know your name, your peril? Weren't you listening? You are of Griaule, daughter. And more so than most, for you have slept at the center of his dreams.

Your entire life has been prelude to this time, and your destiny will not be known until you come to the place from which his dreams arise . . . the dragon's heart." He took her hand. "My name is Amos Mauldry. Captain Amos Mauldry, at your service. I have waited years for you . . . years! I am to prepare you for the consummate moment of your life. I urge you to follow me, to join the company of the Feelys and begin your preparation. But," — he shrugged — "the choice is yours. I will not coerce you more than I have done . . . except to say this. Go with me now, and when you return you will discover that you have nothing to fear of the Willen brothers."

He let loose of her hand and stood gazing at her with calm regard. She would have liked to disregard his words, but they were in such accord with all she had ever felt about her association with the dragon, she found that she could not. "Who," she asked, "are the Feelys?"

He made a disparaging noise. "Harmless creatures. They pass their time copulating and arguing among themselves over the most trivial of matters. Were they not of service to Griaule, keeping him free of certain pests, they would have no use whatsoever. Still, there are worse folk in the world, and they do have moments in which they shine." He shifted impatiently, tapped his cane on the chamber floor. "You'll meet them soon enough. Are you with me or not?"

Grudgingly, her hook at the ready, Catherine followed Mauldry toward the opening at the rear of the chamber and into a narrow, twisting channel illuminated by a pulsing golden light that issued from within Griaule's flesh. This radiance, Mauldry said, derived from the dragon's blood, which, while it did not flow, was subject to fluctuations in brilliance due to changes in its chemistry. Or so he believed. He had regained his light-hearted manner, and as they walked he told Catherine he had captained a cargo ship that plied between Port Chantay and the Pearl Islands.

"We carried livestock, breadfruit, whale oil," he said. "I can't think of much we didn't carry. It was a good life, but hard as hard gets, and after I retired . . . well, I'd never married, and with time on my hands, I figured I owed myself some high times. I decided I'd see the sights, and the sight I most wanted to see was Griaule. I'd heard he was the First Wonder of the World . . . and he was! I was amazed, flabbergasted. I couldn't get enough of seeing him. He was more than a wonder. A miracle, an absolute majesty of a creature. People warned me to keep clear of the mouth, and they were right. But I couldn't stay away. One evening — I was walking along the edge of the mouth — two scalehunters set upon me, beat and robbed me. Left me for dead. And I would have died if it hadn't been for the Feelys." He clucked his tongue. "I suppose I might as well give you some of their background. It can't help but prepare you for them . . . and I admit they need preparing for. They're not in the least agreeable to the eye." He cocked an eye toward Catherine, and after a dozen steps more he said, "Aren't you going to ask me to proceed?"

"You didn't seem to need encouragement," she said.

He chuckled, nodding his approval. "Quite right, quite right." He walked on in silence, his shoulders hunched and head inclined, like an old turtle who'd learned to get about on two legs.

"Well?" said Catherine, growing annoyed.

"I knew you'd ask," he said, and winked at her. "I didn't know who they were myself at first. If I had known I'd have been terrified. There are about five or six hundred in the colony. Their numbers are kept down by childbirth mortality and various other forms of attrition. They're most of them the descendants of a retarded man named Feely who wandered into the mouth almost a thousand years ago. Apparently he was walking near the mouth when flights of birds and swarms of insects began issuing from it. Not just a few, mind you. Entire populations. Wellsir, Feely was badly frightened. He was sure that some terrible beast had chased all these lesser creatures out, and he tried to hide from it. But he was so confused that instead of running away from the mouth, he ran into it and hid in the bushes. He waited for almost a day . . . no beast. The only sign of danger was a muffled thud from deep within the dragon. Finally his curiosity overcame his fear, and he went into the throat." Mauldry hawked and spat. "He felt secure there. More secure than on the outside, at any rate. Doubtless Griaule's doing, that feeling. He needed the Feelys to be happy so they'd settle down and be his exterminators. Anyway, the first thing Feely did was to bring in a madwoman he'd known in Teocinte, and over the years they recruited other madmen who happened along. I was the first sane person they'd brought into the fold. They're extremely chauvinistic regarding the sane. But of course they were directed by Griaule to take me in. He knew you'd need someone to talk to." He prodded the wall with his cane. "And now this is my home. More than a home. It's my truth, my love. To live here is to be transfigured."

"That's a bit hard to swallow," said Catherine.

"Is it, now? You of all those who dwell on the surface should understand the scope of Griaule's virtues. There's no greater security than that he offers, no greater comprehension than that he bestows."

"You make him sound like a god."

Mauldry stopped walking, looking at her askance. The golden light waxed bright, filling in his wrinkles with shadows,

making him appear to be centuries old.
"Well, what do you think he is?" he asked
with an air of mild indignation. "What else
could he be?"

Another ten minutes brought them to
a chamber even more fabulous than the
last. In shape it was oval, like an egg with a
flattened bottom stood on end, an egg
some one hundred and fifty feet high and
a bit more than half that in diameter. It
was lit by the same pulsing golden glow
that had illuminated the channel, but here
the fluctuations were more gradual and
more extreme, ranging from a murky
dimness to a glare approaching that of full
daylight. The upper two thirds of the
chamber wall were obscured by stacked
ranks of small cubicles, leaning together at
rickety angles, a geometry lacking the
precision of the cells of a honeycomb, yet
reminiscent of such, as if the bees that
constructed it had been drunk. The
entrances of the cubicles were draped
with curtains, and lashed to their sides
were ropes, rope ladders, and baskets that
functioned as elevators, several of which
were in use, lowering and lifting men and
women dressed in a style similar to
Mauldry: Catherine was reminded of a

painting she had seen depicting the roof warrens of Port Chantay; but those habitations, while redolent of poverty and despair, had not as did these evoked an impression of squalid degeneracy, of order lapsed into the perverse. The lower portion of the chamber (and it was in this area that the channel emerged) was covered with a motley carpet composed of bolts of silk and satin and other rich fabrics, and seventy or eighty people were strolling and reclining on the gentle slopes. Only the center had been left clear, and there a gaping hole led away into yet another section of the dragon; a system of pipes ran into the hole, and Mauldry later explained that these carried the wastes of the colony into a pit of acids that had once fueled Griaule's fires. The dome of the chamber was choked with mist, the same pale stuff that had been vented from the protuberances in the previous chamber; birds with black wings and red markings on their heads made wheeling flights in and out of it, and frail scarves of mist drifted throughout. There was a sickly sweet odor to the place, and Catherine heard a murmurous rustling that issued from every quarter.

"Well," said Mauldry, making a sweeping gesture with his cane that included the entire chamber. "What do you think of our little colony?"

Some of the Feelys had noticed them and were edging forward in small groups, stopping, whispering agitatedly among themselves, then edging forward again, all with the hesitant curiosity of savages; and although no signal had been given, the curtains over the cubicle entrances were being thrown back, heads were poking forth, and tiny figures were shinnying down the ropes, crowding into baskets, scuttling downward on the rope ladders, hundreds of people beginning to hurry toward her at a pace that brought to mind the panicked swarming of an anthill. And on first glance they seemed alike as ants. Thin and pale and stooped, with sloping, nearly hairless skulls, and weepy eyes and thick-lipped slack mouths, like ugly children in their rotted silks and satins. Closer and closer they came, those in front pushed by the swelling ranks at their rear, and Catherine, unnerved by their stares, ignoring Mauldry's attempts to soothe her, retreated into the channel. Mauldry turned to the Feelys, brandishing his cane as if it were a victor's sword, and cried, "She is here! He has brought her to us at last! She is here!"

His words caused several of those at the front of the press to throw back their heads and loose a whinnying laughter that went higher and higher in pitch as the golden light brightened. Others in the crowd lifted their hands, palms outward, holding them tight to their chests, and made little hops of excitement, and others yet twitched their heads from side to side, cutting their eyes this way and that, their expressions flowing between belligerence and confusion, apparently unsure of what was happening. This exhibition, clearly displaying the Feelys' retardation, the tenuousness of their self-control, dis-mayed Catherine still more. But Mauldry seemed delighted and continued to exhort them, shouting, "She is here," over and over. His outcry came to rule the Feelys, to orchestrate their movements. They began to sway, to repeat his words, slurring them so that their response was in effect a single word, "Shees'eer, Shees'eer," that reverberated through the chamber, acquiring a rolling echo, a hissing sonority, like the rapid breathing of a giant.

The sound washed over Catherine, enfeebling her with its intensity, and she shrank back against the wall of the channel, expecting the Feelys to break ranks and surround her; but they were so absorbed in their chanting, they appeared to have forgotten her. They milled about, bumping into one another, some striking out in anger at those who had impeded their way, others embracing and giggling, engaging in sexual play, but all of them keeping up the chorus of shouts.

Mauldry turned to her, his eyes giving back gleams of the golden light, his face looking in its vacuous glee akin to those of the Feelys, and holding out his hands to her, his tone manifesting the bland sincerity of a priest, he said, "Welcome home."

Three

Catherine was housed in two rooms halfway up the chamber wall, an apartment that adjoined Mauldry's quarters and was furnished with a rich carpeting of silks and furs and embroidered pillows; on the walls, also draped in these materials, hung a mirror with a gem-studded frame and two oil paintings — this bounty, said Mauldry, all part of Griaule's horde, the bulk of which lay in a cave west of the valley, its location known only to the Feelys. One of the rooms contained a large basin for bathing, but since water was at a premium — being collected from points at which it seeped in through the scales — she was permitted one bath a week and no more. Still, the apartment and the general living conditions were on a par with those in Hangtown, and had it not been for the Feelys, Catherine might have felt at home. But except in the case of the woman Leitha, who served her meals and cleaned, she could not overcome her revulsion at their inbred appearance and demented manner. They seemed to be responding to stimuli that she could not perceive, stopping now and then to cock an ear to an inaudible call or to stare at some invisible disturbance in the air. They scurried up and down the ropes to no apparent purpose, laughing and chattering, and they engaged in mass copulations at the bottom of the chamber. They spoke a mongrel dialect that she could barely understand, and they would hang on ropes outside her apartment, arguing, offering criticism of one another's dress and behavior, picking at the most insignificant of flaws and judging them according to an intricate code whose niceties Catherine was unable to master. They would follow her wherever she went, never sharing the same basket, but descending or ascending alongside her, staring, shrinking away if she turned her gaze upon them. With their foppish rags, their jewels, their childish pettiness and

jealousies, they both irritated and frightened her; there was a tremendous tension
in the way they looked at her, and she had
the idea that at any moment they might
lose their awe of her and attack.

She kept to her rooms those first
weeks, brooding, trying to invent some
means of escape, her solitude broken only
by Leitha's ministrations and Mauldry's
visits. He came twice daily and would sit
among the pillows, declaiming upon
Griaule's majesty, his truth. She did not
enjoy the visits. The righteous quaver in
his voice aroused her loathing, reminding
her of the mendicant priests who passed
now and then through Hangtown, leaving
bastards and empty purses in their wake.
She found his conversation for the most
part boring, and when it did not bore, she
found it disturbing in its constant refer-
ences to her time of trial at the dragon's
heart. She had no doubt that Griaule was
at work in her life. The longer she
remained in the colony, the more vivid her
dreams became and the more certain she
grew that his purpose was somehow
aligned with her presence there. But the
pathetic condition of the Feelys shed a
wan light on her old fantasies of a destiny

entwined with the dragon's, and she began to see herself in that wan light, to experience a revulsion at her fecklessness equal to that she felt toward those around her.

"You are our salvation," Mauldry told her one day as she sat sewing herself a new pair of trousers — she refused to dress in the gilt and satin rags preferred by the Feelys. "Only you can know the mystery of the dragon's heart, only you can inform us of his deepest wish for us. We've known this for years."

Seated amid the barbaric disorder of silks and furs, Catherine looked out through a gap in the curtains, watching the waning of the golden light. "You hold me prisoner," she said. "Why should I help you?"

"Would you leave us, then?" Mauldry asked. "What of the Willens?"

"I doubt they're still waiting for me. Even if they are, it's only a matter of which death I prefer, a lingering one here or a swift one at their hands."

Mauldry fingered the gold knob of his cane. "You're right," he said. "The Willens are no longer a menace."

She glanced up at him.

"They died the moment you went

down out of Griaule's mouth," he said. "He sent his creatures to deal with them, knowing you were his at long last."

Catherine remembered the shouts she'd heard while walking down the incline of the throat. "What creatures?"

"That's of no importance," said Mauldry. "What is important is that you apprehend the subtlety of his power, his absolute mastery and control over your thoughts, your being."

"Why?" she asked. "Why is that important?" He seemed to be struggling to explain himself, and she laughed. "Lost touch with your god, Mauldry? Won't he supply the appropriate cant?"

Mauldry composed himself. "It is for you, not I, to understand why you are here. You must explore Griaule, study the miraculous workings of his flesh, involve yourself in the intricate order of his being."

In frustration, Catherine punched at a pillow. "If you don't let me go, I'll die! This place will kill me. I won't be around long enough to do any exploring."

"Oh, but you will." Mauldry favored her with an unctuous smile. "That, too, is known to us."

Ropes creaked, and a moment later the

curtains parted, and Leitha, a young woman in a gown of watered blue taffeta, whose bodice pushed up the pale nubs of her breasts, entered bearing Catherine's dinner tray. She set down the tray. "Be mo', ma'am?" she said. "Or mus' I later c'meah." She gazed fixedly at Catherine, her close-set brown eyes blinking, fingers plucking at the folds of her gown.

"Whatever you want," Catherine said.

Leitha continued to stare at her, and only when Mauldry spoke sharply to her, did she turn and leave.

Catherine looked down disconsolately at the tray and noticed that in addition to the usual fare of greens and fruit (gathered from the dragon's mouth) there were several slices of underdone meat, whose reddish hue appeared identical to the color of Griaule's flesh. "What's this?" she asked, poking at one of the slices.

"The hunters were successful today," said Mauldry. "Every so often hunting parties are sent into the digestive tract. It's quite dangerous, but there are beasts there that can injure Griaule. It serves him that we hunt them, and their flesh nourishes us." He leaned forward, studying her face. "Another party is going

out tomorrow. Perhaps you'd care to join
them. I can arrange it if you wish. You'll
be well protected."

Catherine's initial impulse was to reject
the invitation, but then she thought that
this might offer an opportunity for escape;
in fact, she realized that to play upon
Mauldry's tendencies, to evince interest in
a study of the dragon, would be a wise
move. The more she learned about
Griaule's geography, the greater chance
there would be that she would find a way
out.

"You said it was dangerous . . . How
dangerous?"

"For you? Not in the least. Griaule
would not harm you. But for the hunting
party, well . . . lives will be lost."

"And they're going out tomorrow?"

"Perhaps the next day as well. We're
not sure how extensive an infestation is
involved."

"What kind of beast are you talking
about?"

"Serpents of a sort."

Catherine's enthusiasm was dimmed,
but she saw no other means of taking
action. "Very well. I'll go with them
tomorrow."

"Wonderful, wonderful!" It took Mauldry three tries to heave himself up from the cushion, and when at last he managed to stand, he leaned on his cane, breathing heavily. "I'll come for you early in the morning,"

"You're going, too? You don't seem up to the exertion."

Mauldry chuckled. "It's true, I'm an old man. But where you're concerned, daughter, my energies are inexhaustible." He performed a gallant bow and hobbled from the room.

Not long after he had left, Leitha returned. She drew a second curtain across the entrance, cutting the light, even at its most brilliant, to a dim effusion. Then she stood by the entrance, eyes fixed on Catherine. "Wan' mo' fum Leitha?" she asked.

The question was not a formality. Leitha had made it plain by touches and other signs that Catherine had but to ask and she would come to her as a lover. Her deformities masked by the shadowy air, she had the look of a pretty young girl dressed for a dance, and for a moment, in the grip of loneliness and despair, watching Leitha alternately brightening and merging with gloom, listening to the unceasing murmur of the Feelys from without, aware in full of the tribal strangeness of the colony and her utter lack of connection, Catherine felt a bizarre arousal. But the moment passed, and she was disgusted with herself, with her weakness, and angry at Leitha and this degenerate place that was eroding her humanity. "Get out," she said coldly, and when Leitha hesitated, she shouted the command, sending the girl stumbling backwards from the room. Then she turned onto her stomach, her face pressed into a pillow, expecting to cry, feeling the pressure of a sob building in her chest; but the sob never manifested, and she lay there, knowing her emptiness, feeling that she was no longer worthy of even her own tears.

Behind one of the cubicles in the lower half of the chamber was hidden the entrance to a wide circular passage ringed by ribs of cartilage, and it was along this passage the next morning that Catherine and Mauldry, accompanied by thirty male Feelys, set out upon the hunt. They were

armed with swords and bore torches to
light the way, for here Griaule's veins were
too deeply embedded to provide illumination; they walked in a silence broken only
by coughs and the soft scraping of their
footsteps. The silence, such a contrast
from the Feelys' usual chatter, unsettled
Catherine, and the flaring and guttering of
the torches, the apparition of a backlit pale
face turned toward her, the tingling acidic
scent that grew stronger and stronger, all
this assisted her impression that they were
lost souls treading some byway in Hell.

Their angle of descent increased, and
shortly thereafter they reached a spot
from which Catherine had a view of a
black distance shot through with intricate
networks of fine golden skeins, like
spiderwebs of gold in a night sky. Mauldry
told her to wait, and the torches of the
hunting party moved off, making it clear
that they had come to a large chamber;
but she did not understand just how large
until a fire suddenly bloomed, bursting
into towering flames: an enormous bonfire
composed of sapling trunks and entire
bushes. The size of the fire was impressive
in itself, but the immense cavity of the
stomach that it partially revealed was

more impressive yet. It could not have
been less than two hundred yards long,
and was walled with folds of thin whitish
skin figured by lacings and branchings of
veins, attached to curving ribs covered
with even thinner skin that showed their
every articulation. A quarter of the way
across the cavity, the floor declined into a
sink brimming with a dark liquid, and it
was along a section of the wall close to the
sink that the bonfire had been lit, its smoke
billowing up toward a bruised patch of
skin some fifty feet in circumference with a
tattered rip at the center. As Catherine
watched the entire patch began to
undulate. The hunting party gathered
beneath it, ranged around the bonfire,
their swords raised. Then, with ponderous
slowness a length of thick white tubing
was extruded from the rip, a gigantic
worm that lifted its blind head above the
hunting party, opened a mouth fringed
with palps to expose a dark red maw and
emitted a piercing squeal that touched off
echoes and made Catherine put her hands
to her ears. More and more of the worm's
body emerged from the stomach wall, and
she marveled at the courage of the
hunting party, who maintained their

ground. The worm's squealing became unbearably loud as smoke enveloped it; it lashed about, twisting and probing at the air with its head, and then, with an even louder cry, it fell across the bonfire, writhing, sending up showers of sparks. It rolled out of the fire, crushing several of the party; the others set to with their swords, hacking in a frenzy at the head, painting streaks of dark blood over the corpse-pale skin. Catherine realized that she had pressed her fists to her cheeks and was screaming, so involved was she in the battle. The worm's blood spattered the floor of the cavity, its skin was charred and blistered from the flames, and its head was horribly slashed, the flesh hanging in ragged strips. But it continued to squeal, humping up great sections of its body, forming an arch over groups of attackers and dropping down upon them. A third of the hunting party lay motionless, their limbs sprawled in graceless attitudes, the remnants of the bonfire — heaps of burning branches — scattered among them; the rest stabbed and sliced at the increasingly torpid worm, dancing away from its lunges. At last the worm lifted half its body off the floor, its head held high, silent for a moment, swaying with the languor of a mesmerized serpent. It let out a cry like the whistle of a monstrous tea kettle, a cry that seemed to fill the cavity with its fierce vibrations, and fell, twisting once and growing still, its maw half-open, palps twitching in the register of some final internal function.

The hunting party collapsed around it, winded, drained, some leaning on their swords. Shocked by the suddenness of the silence, Catherine went a few steps out into the cavity, Mauldry at her shoulder. She hesitated, then moved forward again, thinking that some of the party might need tending. But those who had fallen were dead, their limbs broken, blood showing on their mouths. She walked alongside the worm. The thickness of its body was three times her height, the skin glistening and warped by countless tiny puckers and tinged with a faint bluish cast that made it all the more ghastly.

"What are you thinking?" Mauldry asked.

Catherine shook her head. No thoughts would come to her. It was as if the process of thought itself had been cancelled by the enormity of what she had witnessed. She had always supposed that she had a fair idea of Griaule's scope, his complexity, but now she understood that whatever she had once believed had been inadequate, and she struggled to acclimate to this new perspective. There was a commotion behind her. Members of the hunting party were hacking slabs of meat from the worm. Mauldry draped an arm about her, and by that contact she became aware that she was trembling.

"Come along," he said. "I'll take you home."

"To my room, you mean?" Her bitterness resurfaced, and she threw off his arm.

"Perhaps you'll never think of it as home," he said. "Yet nowhere is there is place more suited to you." He signaled to one of the hunting party, who came toward them, stopping to light a dead torch from a pile of burning branches.

With a dismal laugh, Catherine said, "I'm beginning to find it irksome how you claim to know so much about me."

"It's not you I claim to know," he said, "though it has been given me to understand something of your purpose. But," — he rapped the tip of his cane against the floor of the cavity — "he by whom you are most known, him I know well."

Four

Catherine made three escape attempts during the next two months, and thereafter gave up on the enterprise; with hundreds of eyes watching her, there was no point in wasting energy. For almost six months following the final attempt she became dispirited and refused to leave her rooms. Her health suffered, her thoughts paled, and she lay abed for hours, reliving her life in Hangtown, which she came to view as a model of joy and contentment. Her inactivity caused loneliness to bear in upon her. Mauldry tried his best to entertain her, but his mystical obsession with Griaule made him incapable of offering the consolation of a true friend. And so, without friends or lovers, without even an enemy, she sank into a welter of self-pity and began to toy with the idea of suicide. The prospect of never seeing the sun again, of attending no more carnivals at Teocinte . . . it seemed too much to endure. But either she was not brave enough or not sufficiently foolish to take her own life, and deciding that no matter how vile or delimiting the circumstance, it promised more than eternal darkness, she gave herself to the one occupation the Feelys would permit her: the exploration and study of Griaule.

Like one of those enormous Tibetan sculptures of the Buddha constructed within a tower only a trifle larger than the sculpture itself, Griaule's unbeating heart was a dimpled golden shape as vast as a cathedral and was enclosed within a chamber whose walls left a gap six feet wide around the organ. The chamber could be reached by passing through a vein that had ruptured long ago and was now a wrinkled brown tube just big enough for Catherine to crawl along it; to make this transit and then emerge into that narrow space beside the heart was an intensely claustrophobic experience, and it took her a long, long while to get used to the process. Even after she had grown accustomed to this, it was still difficult for her to adjust to the peculiar climate at the heart. The air was thick with a heated stinging scent that reminded her of the brimstone stink left by a lightning stroke, and there was an atmosphere of imminence, a stillness and tension redolent of some chthonic disturbance that might strike at any moment. The blood at the heart did not merely fluctuate (and here the fluctuations were erratic, varying both in range of brilliance and rapidity of change); it circulated — the movement due to variations in heat and pressure — through a series of convulsed inner chambers, and this eddying in conjunction with the flickering brilliance threw patterns of light and shadow on the heart wall, patterns as complex and fanciful as arabesques that drew her eye in. Staring at them, Catherine began to be able to predict what configurations would next appear and to apprehend a logic to their progression; it was nothing that she could put into words, but watching the play of light and shadow produced in her emotional responses that seemed keyed to the shifting patterns and allowed her to make crude guesses as to the heart's workings. She learned that if she stared too long at the patterns, dreams would take her, dreams notable for their vividness, and one particularly notable in that it recurred again and again.

The dream began with a sunrise, the solar disc edging up from the southern horizon, its rays spearing toward a coast strewn with great black rocks that protruded from the shallows, and perched upon them were sleeping dragons; as the sun warmed them, light flaring on their scales, they grumbled and lifted their heads and with the snapping sound of huge sails filling with wind, they unfolded their leathery wings and went soaring up into an indigo sky flecked with stars arranged into strange constellations, wheeling and roaring their exultation . . . all but one dragon, who flew only a brief arc before coming disjointed in mid-flight and dropping like a stone into the water, vanishing beneath the waves. It was an awesome thing to see, this tumbling flight, the wings billowing, tearing, the fanged mouth open, claws grasping for purchase in the air. But despite its beauty, the dream seemed to have little relevance to Griaule's situation. He was in no danger of falling, that much was certain. Never-theless, the frequency of the dream's recurrence persuaded Catherine that something must be amiss, that perhaps Griaule feared an attack of the sort that had stricken the flying dragon. With this in mind she began to inspect the heart, using her hooks to clamber up the steep slopes of the chamber walls, sometimes hanging upside down like a blond spider above the glowing, flickering organ. But she could find nothing out of order, no imperfections — at least as far as she could determine — and the sole result of the inspection was that the dream stopped occurring and was replaced by a simpler dream in which she watched the chest of a sleeping dragon contract and expand. She could make no sense of it, and although the dream continued to recur, she paid less and less attention to it.

Mauldry, who had been expecting mir-aculous insights from her, was depressed when none were forthcoming. "Perhaps I've been wrong all these years," he said. "Or senile. Perhaps I'm growing senile."

A few months earlier, Catherine, locked into bitterness and resentment, might have seconded his opinion out of spite; but her studies at the heart had soothed her, infused her both with calm resignation and some compassion for her jailers — they could not, after all, be blamed for their pitiful condition — and she said to Mauldry, "I've only begun to learn. It's likely to take a long time before I understand what he wants. And that's in keeping with his nature, isn't it? That nothing happens quickly?"

"I suppose you're right," he said glumly.

"Of course I am," she said. "Sooner or later there'll be a revelation. But a creature like Griaule doesn't yield his secrets to a casual glance. Just give me time."

And oddly enough, though she had spoken these words to cheer Mauldry, they seemed to ring true.

She had started her explorations with minimal enthusiasm, but Griaule's scope was so extensive, his populations of parasites and symbiotes so exotic and intriguing, her passion for knowledge was fired and over the next six years she grew zealous in her studies, using them to compensate for the emptiness of her life. With Mauldry ever at her side, accompanied by small groups of the Feelys, she mapped the interior of the dragon, stopping short of penetrating the skull, warned off from that region by a premonition of danger. She sent several of the more intelligent Feelys into Teocinte, where they acquired beakers and flasks and books and writing materials that enabled her to build a primitive laboratory for chemical analysis. She discovered that the egg-shaped chamber occupied by the colony would — had the dragon been fully alive — be pumped full of acids and gasses by the contraction of the heart muscle, flooding the channel, mingling in the adjoining chamber with yet another liquid, forming a volatile mixture that Griaule's breath would — if he so desired — kindle into flame; if he did not so desire, the expansion of the heart would empty the chamber. From these liquids she derived a potent narcotic that she named brianine after her nemesis, and from a lichen growing on the outer surface of the lungs, she derived a powerful stimulant. She catalogued the dragon's myriad flora and fauna, covering the walls of her rooms with lists and charts and notations on their behaviors. Many of the animals were either familiar to her or variants of familiar forms. Spiders, bats, swallows, and the like. But as was the case on the dragon's surface, a few of them testified to his otherworldly origins, and perhaps the most curious of them was Catherine's metahex (her designation for it), a creature with six identical bodies that thrived in the stomach acids. Each body was approximately the size and color of a worn penny, fractionally more dense than a jellyfish, ringed with cilia, and all were in a constant state of agitation. She had at first assumed the metahex to be six creatures, a species that traveled in sixes, but had begun to suspect otherwise when — upon killing one for the purposes of dissection — the other five bodies had also died. She had initiated a series of experiments that involved menacing and killing hundreds of the things, and had ascertained that the bodies were connected by some sort of field — one whose presence she deduced by process of observation — that permitted the essence of the creature to switch back and forth between the bodies, utilizing the ones it did not occupy as a unique form of camouflage. But even the metahex seemed ordinary when compared to the ghostvine, a plant that she discovered grew in one place alone, a small cavity near the base of the skull.

None of the colony would approach that region, warned away by the same sense of danger that had afflicted Catherine, and it was presumed that should one venture too close to the brain, Griaule would mobilize some of his more deadly inhabitants to deal with the interloper. But Catherine felt secure in approaching the cavity, and leaving Mauldry and her escort of Feelys behind, she climbed the steep channel that led up to it, lighting her way with a torch, and entered through an aperture not much wider than her hips. Once inside, seeing that the place was lit by veins of golden blood that branched across the ceiling, flickering like the blown flame of a candle, she extinguished the torch; she noticed with surprise that except for the ceiling, the entire cavity — a boxy space some twenty feet long, about eight feet in height — was fettered with vines whose leaves were dark green, glossy, with complex veination and tips that ended in miniscule hollow tubes. She was winded from the climb, more winded — she thought — than she should have been, and she sat down against the wall to catch her breath; then, feeling drowsy, she closed her eyes for a moment's rest. She came alert to the sound of Mauldry's voice shouting her name. Still drowsy, annoyed by his impatience, she called out, "I just want to rest a few minutes!"

"A few minutes?" he cried. "You've been there three days! What's going on? Are you all right?"

"That's ridiculous!" She started to come to her feet, then sat back, stunned by the sight of a naked woman with long blond hair curled up in a corner not ten feet away, nestled so close to the cavity wall that the tips of leaves half-covered her body and obscured her face.

"Catherine!" Mauldry shouted. "Answer me!"

"I . . . I'm all right! Just a minute!"

The woman stirred and made a complaining noise.

"Catherine!"

"I said I'm all right!"

The woman stretched out her legs; on her right hip was a fine pink scar, hook-shaped, identical to the scar on Catherine's hip, evidence of a childhood fall. And on the back of the right knee, a patch of raw, puckered skin, the product of an acid burn she'd suffered the year before. She was astonished by the sight of these markings, but when the woman sat up and Catherine understood that she was staring at her twin — identical not only in feature, but also in expression, wearing a resigned look that she had glimpsed many times in her mirror — her astonishment turned to fright. She could have sworn she felt the muscles of the woman's face shifting as the expression changed into one of pleased recognition, and in spite of her fear, she had a vague sense of the woman's emotions, of her burgeoning hope and elation.

"Sister," said the woman; she glanced down at her body, and Catherine had a momentary flash of doubled vision, watching the woman's head decline and seeing as well naked breasts and belly from the perspective of the woman's eyes. Her vision returned to normal, and she looked at the woman's face . . . *her* face. Though she had studied herself in the mirror each morning for years, she had never had such a clear perception of the changes that life inside the dragon had wrought upon her. Fine lines bracketed her lips, and the beginnings of crows feet radiated from the corners of her eyes. Her cheeks had hollowed, and this made her cheekbones appear sharper; the set of her mouth seemed harder, more determined. The high gloss and perfection of her youthful beauty had been marred far more than she had thought, and this dismayed her. However, the most remarkable change — the one that most struck her — was not embodied by any one detail but in the overall character of the face, in that it exhibited character, for — she realized — prior to entering the dragon it had displayed very little, and what little it *had* displayed had been evidence of indulgence. It troubled her to have this knowledge of the fool she had been thrust upon her with such poignancy.

As if the woman had been listening to her thoughts, she held out her hand and said, "Don't punish yourself, sister. We are all victims of our past."

"What are you?" Catherine asked, pulling back. She felt the woman was a danger to her, though she was not sure why.

"I am you." Again the woman reached out to touch her, and again Catherine shifted away. The woman's face was smiling, but Catherine felt the wash of her frustration and noticed that the woman had leaned forward only a few degrees, remaining in contact with the leaves of the vines as if there were some attachment between them that she could not break.

"I doubt that." Catherine was fascinated, but she was beginning to be swayed by the intuition that the woman's touch would harm her.

"But I am!" the woman insisted. "And something more, besides."

"What more?"

"The plant extracts essences," said the woman. "Infinitely small constructs of the flesh from which it creates a likeness free of the imperfections of your body. And since the seeds of your future are embodied by these essences, though they are unknown to you, I know them . . . for now."

"For now?"

The woman's tone had become desperate. "There's a connection between us . . . surely you feel it?"

"Yes."

"To live, to complete that connection, I must touch you. And once I do, this knowledge of the future will be lost to me.

I will be as you . . . though separate. But don't worry. I won't interfere with you, I'll live my own life." She leaned forward again, and Catherine saw that some of the leaves were affixed to her back, the hollow tubes at their tips adhering to the skin. Once again she had an awareness of danger, a growing apprehension that the woman's touch would drain her of some vital substance.

"If you know my future," she said, "then tell me . . . will I ever escape Griaule?"

Mauldry chose this moment to call out to her, and she soothed him by saying that she was taking some cuttings, that she would be down soon. She repeated her question, and the woman said, "Yes, yes, you will leave the dragon," and tried to grasp her hand. "Don't be afraid. I won't harm you."

The woman's flesh was sagging, and Catherine felt the eddying of her fear.

"Please!" she said, holding out both hands. "Only your touch will sustain me. Without it, I'll die!"

But Catherine refused to trust her.

"You must believe me!" cried the woman. "I am your sister! My blood is yours, my memories!" The flesh upon her arms had sagged into billows like the flesh of an old woman, and her face was becoming jowly, grossly distorted. "Oh, please! Remember the time with Stel below the wing . . . you were a maiden. The wind was blowing thistles down from Griaule's back like a rain of silver. And remember the gala in Teocinte? Your sixteenth birthday. You wore a mask of orange blossoms and gold wire, and three men asked for your hand. For God's sake, Catherine! Listen to me! The major . . . don't you remember him? The young major? You were in love with him, but you didn't follow your heart. You were afraid of love, you didn't trust what you felt because you never trusted yourself in those days."

The connection between them was fading, and Catherine steeled herself against the woman's entreaties, which had begun to move her more than a little bit. The woman slumped down, her features blurring, a horrid sight, like the melting of a wax figure, and then, an even more horrid sight, she smiled, her lips appearing to dissolve away from teeth that were themselves dissolving.

"I understand," said the woman in a

frail voice, and gave a husky, glutinous laugh. "Now I see."

"What is it?" Catherine asked. But the woman collapsed, rolling onto her side, and the process of deterioration grew more rapid; within the span of a few minutes she had dissipated into a gelatinous grayish white puddle that retained the rough outline of her form. Catherine was both appalled and relieved; however, she couldn't help feeling some remorse, uncertain whether she had acted in self-defense or through cowardice had damned a creature who was by nature no more reprehensible than herself. While the woman had been alive — if that was the proper word — Catherine had been mostly afraid, but now she marveled at the apparition, at the complexity of a plant that could produce even the semblance of a human. And the woman had been, she thought, something more vital than mere likeness. How else could she have known her memories? Or could memory, she wondered, have a physiological basis? She forced herself to take samples of the woman's remains, of the vines, with an eye toward exploring the mystery. But she doubted that the heart of such an intricate mystery would be accessible to her primitive instruments. This was to prove a self-fulfilling prophecy, because she really did not want to know the secrets of the ghostvine, leery as to what might be brought to light concerning her own nature, and with the passage of time, although she thought of it often and sometimes discussed the phenomena with Mauldry, she eventually let the matter drop.

Five

Though the temperature never changed, though neither rain nor snow fell, though the fluctuations of the golden light remained consistent in their rhythms, the seasons were registered inside the dragon by migrations of birds, the weaving of cocoons, the birth of millions of insects at once; and it was by these signs that Catherine — nine years after entering Griaule's mouth — knew it to be autumn when she fell in love. The three years prior to this had been characterized by a slackening of her zeal, a gradual wearing down of her enthusiasm for scientific knowledge, and this tendency became marked after the death of Captain Mauldry from natural causes; without him to serve as a buffer between her and the

Feelys, she was overwhelmed by their inanity, their woeful aspect. In truth, there was not much left to learn. Her maps were complete, her specimens and notes filled several rooms, and while she continued her visits to the dragon's heart, she no longer sought to interpret the dreams, using them instead to pass the boring hours. Again she grew restless and began to consider escape. Her life was being wasted, she believed, and she wanted to return to the world, to engage more vital opportunities than those available to her in Griaule's many-chambered prison. It was not that she was ungrateful for the experience. Had she managed to escape shortly after her arrival, she would have returned to a life of meaningless frivolity; but now, armed with knowledge, aware of her strengths and weaknesses, possessed of ambition and a heightened sense of morality, she thought she would be able to accomplish something of importance. But before she could determine whether or not escape was possible, there was a new arrival at the colony, a man whom a group of Feelys — while gathering berries near the mouth — had found lying unconscious and had borne to safety.

The man's name was John Colmacos, and he was in his early thirties, a botanist from the university at Port Chantay who had been abandoned by his guides when he insisted on entering the mouth and had subsequently been mauled by apes that had taken up residence in the mouth. He was lean, rawboned, with powerful, thick-fingered hands and fine brown hair that would never stay combed. His long-jawed, horsey face struck a bargain between homely and distinctive, and was stamped with a perpetually inquiring expression as if he were a bit perplexed by everything he saw, and his blue eyes were large and intricate, the irises flecked with green and hazel, appearing surprisingly delicate in contrast to the rest of him.

Catherine, happy to have rational company, especially that of a professional in her vocation, took charge of nursing him back to health — he had suffered fractures of the arm and ankle, and was badly cut about the face; and in the course of this she began to have fantasies about him as a lover. She had never met a man with his gentleness of manner, his lack of pretense, and she found it most surprising that he wasn't concerned with trying to impress her. Her conception of men had been limited to the soldiers of Teocinte, the thugs of Hangtown, and everything about John fascinated her. For awhile she tried to deny her feelings, telling herself that she would have fallen in love with almost anyone under the circumstances, afraid that by loving she would only increase her dissatisfaction with her prison; and, too, there was the realization that this was doubtless another of Griaule's manipulations, his attempt to make her content with her lot, to replace Mauldry with a lover. But she couldn't deny that under any circumstance she would have been attracted to John Colmacos for many reasons, not the least of which was his respect for her work with Griaule, for how she had handled adversity. Nor could she deny that the attraction was mutual. That was clear. Although there were awkward moments, there was no mooniness between them; they were both watching what was happening.

"This is amazing," he said one day, while going through one of her notebooks, lying on a pile of furs in her apartment. "It's hard to believe you haven't had training."

A flush spread over her cheeks. "Anyone in my shoes, with all that time, nothing else to do, they would have done no less."

He set down the notebook and measured her with a stare that caused her to lower her eyes. "You're wrong," he said. "Most people would have fallen apart. I can't think of anybody else who could have managed all this. You're remarkable."

She felt oddly incompetent in the light of this judgment, as if she had accorded him ultimate authority and were receiving the sort of praise that a wise adult might bestow upon an inept child who had done well for once. She wanted to explain to him that everything she had done had been a kind of therapy, a hobby to stave off despair; but she didn't know how to put this into words without sounding awkward and falsely modest, and so she merely said, "Oh," and busied herself with preparing a dose of brianine to take away the pain in his ankle.

"You're embarrassed," he said. "I'm sorry . . . I didn't mean to make you uncomfortable."

"I'm not . . . I mean, I . . . " She laughed.

"I'm still not accustomed to talking."

He said nothing, smiling.

"What is it?" she said, defensive, feeling that he was making fun of her.

"What do you mean?"

"Why are you smiling?"

"I could frown," he said, "if that would make you comfortable."

Irritated, she bent to her task, mixing paste in a brass goblet studded with uncut emeralds, then molding it into a pellet.

"That was a joke," he said.

"I know."

"What's the matter?"

She shook her head. "Nothing."

"Look," he said. "I don't want to make you uncomfortable . . . I really don't. What am I doing wrong?"

She sighed, exasperated with herself. "It's not you," she said. "I just can't get used to you being here, that's all."

From without came the babble of some Feelys lowering on ropes toward the chamber floor.

"I can understand that," he said. "I . . . " He broke off, looked down and fingered the edge of the notebook.

"What were you going to say?"

He threw back his head, laughed. "Do

you see how we're acting? Explaining ourselves constantly . . . as if we could hurt
each other by saying the wrong word."

She glanced over at him, met his eyes,
then looked away.

"What I meant was, we're not that
fragile," he said, and then, as if by way of
clarification, he hastened to add: "We're
not that . . . vulnerable to one another."

He held her stare for a moment, and
this time it was he who looked away and
Catherine who smiled.

If she hadn't known she was in love,
she would have suspected as much from
the change in her attitude toward the
dragon. She seemed to be seeing
everything anew. Her wonder at Griaule's
size and strangeness had been restored,
and she delighted in displaying his
marvelous features to John — the orioles
and swallows that never once had flown
under the sun, the glowing heart, the cavity
where the ghostvine grew (though she
would not linger there), and a tiny
chamber close to the heart lit not by
Griaule's blood but by thousands of
luminous white spiders that shifted and
crept across the blackness of the ceiling,
like a night sky whose constellations had

come to life. It was in this chamber that they engaged in their first intimacy, a kiss from which Catherine — after initially letting herself be swept away — pulled back, disoriented by the powerful sensations flooding her body, sensations both familiar and unnatural in that she hadn't experienced them for so long, and startled by the suddenness with which her fantasies had become real. Flustered, she ran from the chamber, leaving John, who was still hobbled by his injuries, to limp back to the colony alone.

She hid from him most of that day sitting with her knees drawn up on a patch of peach-colored silk near the hole at the center of the colony's floor, immersed in the bustle and gabble of the Feelys as they promenaded in their decaying finery. Though for the most part they were absorbed in their own pursuits, some sensed her mood and gathered around her, touching her, making the whimpering noises that among them passed for expressions of tenderness. Their pasty doglike faces ringed her, uniformly sad, and as if sadness were contagious, she started to cry. At first her tears seemed the product of her inability to cope with

love, and then it seemed she was crying
over the poor thing of her life, the
haplessness of her days inside the body of
the dragon; but she came to feel that her
sadness was one with Griaule's, that this
feeling of gloom and entrapment reflected
his essential mood, and that thought
stopped her tears. She'd never considered
the dragon an object deserving of
sympathy, and she did not now consider
him such; but perceiving him imprisoned
in a web of ancient magic, and the Chinese
puzzle of lesser magics and imprison-
ments that derived from that original
event, she felt foolish for having cried.
Everything, she realized, even the happiest
of occurrences, might be a cause for tears
if you failed to see it in terms of the world
that you inhabited; however, if you
managed to achieve a balanced perspective, you saw that although sadness could
result from every human action, that you
had to seize the opportunities for effective
action which came your way and not
question them, no matter how unrealistic
or futile they might appear. Just as Griaule
had done by finding a way to utilize his
power while immobilized. She laughed to
think of herself emulating Griaule even in

this abstract fashion, and several of the Feelys standing beside her echoed her laughter. One of the males, an old man with tufts of gray hair poking up from his pallid skull, shuffled near, picking at a loose button on his stiff, begrimed coat of silver-embroidered satin.

"Cat'rine mus' be easy sweetly, now?" he said. "No mo' bad t'ing?"

"No," she said. "No more bad thing."

On the other side of the hole a pile of naked Feelys were writhing together in the clumsiness of foreplay, men trying to penetrate men, getting angry, slapping one another, then lapsing into giggles when they found a woman and figured out the proper procedure. Once this would have disgusted her, but no more. Judged by the attitudes of a place not their own, perhaps the Feelys were disgusting; but this *was* their place, and Catherine's place as well, and accepting that at last, she stood and walked toward the nearest basket. The old man hustled after her, fingering his lapels in a parody of self-importance, and, as if he were the functionary of her mood, he announced to everyone they encountered, "No mo' bad t'ing, no mo' bad t'ing."

Riding up in the basket was like passing in front of a hundred tiny stages upon which scenes from the same play was being performed — pale figures slumped on silks, playing with gold and bejeweled baubles — and gazing around her, ignoring the stink, the dilapidation, she felt she was looking out upon an exotic kingdom. Always before she had been impressed by its size and grotesqueness; but now she was struck by its richness, and she wondered whether the Feelys' style of dress was inadvertent or if Griaule's subtlety extended to the point of clothing this human refuse in the rags of dead courtiers and kings. She felt exhilarated, joyful; but as the basket lurched near the level on which her rooms were located, she became nervous. It had been so long since she had been with a man, and she was worried that she might not be suited to him . . . then she recalled that she'd been prone to these worries even in the days when she had been with a new man every week.

She lashed the basket to a peg, stepped out onto the walkway outside her rooms, took a deep breath and pushed through the curtains, pulled them shut behind her. John was asleep, the furs pulled up to his chest. In the fading half-light, his face — dirtied by a few days' growth of beard — looked sweetly mysterious and rapt, like the face of saint at meditation, and she thought it might be best to let him sleep; but that, she realized, was a signal of her nervousness, not of compassion. The only thing to do was to get it over with, to pass through nervousness as quickly as possible and learn what there was to learn. She stripped off her trousers, her shirt, and stood for a second above him, feeling giddy, frail, as if she'd stripped off much more than a few ounces of fabric. Then she eased in beneath the furs, pressing the length of her body to his. He stirred but didn't wake, and this delighted her; she liked the idea of having him in her clutches, of coming to him in the middle of a dream, and she shivered with the apprehension of gleeful, childish power. He tossed, turned onto his side to face her, still asleep, and she pressed closer, marveling at how ready she was, how open to him. He muttered something, and as she nestled against him, he grew hard, his erection pinned between their bellies. Cautiously, she lifted her right knee atop his hip, guided him between her legs and moved her hips back and forth, rubbing against him, slowly, slowly, teasing herself with little bursts of pleasure. His eyelids twitched, blinked open, and he stared at her, his eyes looking black and wet, his skin stained a murky gold in the dimness. "Catherine," he said, and she gave a soft laugh, because her name seemed a power the way he had spoken it. His fingers hooked into the plump meat of her hips as he pushed and prodded at her, trying to find the right angle. Her head fell back, her eyes closed, concentrating on the feeling that centered her dizziness and heat, and then he was inside her, going deep with a single thrust, beginning to make love to her, and she said, "Wait, wait," holding him immobile, afraid for an instant, feeling too much, a black wave of sensation building, threatening to wash her away.

"What's wrong?" he whispered. "Do you want . . . "

"Just wait . . . just for a bit." She rested her forehead against his, trembling, amazed by the difference that he made in her body; one moment she felt buoyant, as if their connection had freed her from the restraints of gravity, and the next moment — whenever he shifted or eased fractionally deeper — she would feel as if all his weight were pouring inside her and she was sinking into the cool silks.

"Are you all right?"

"Mmm." She opened her eyes, saw his face inches away and was surprised that he didn't appear unfamiliar.

"What is it?" he asked.

"I was just thinking."

"About what?"

"I was wondering who you were, and when I looked at you, it was as if I already knew." She traced the line of his upper lip with her forefinger. "Who are you?"

"I thought you knew already."

"Maybe . . . but I don't know anything specific. Just that you were a professor."

"You want to know specifics?"

"Yes."

"I was an unruly child," he said. "I refused to eat onion soup, I never washed behind my ears."

His grasp tightened on her hips, and he thrust inside her, a few slow, delicious movements, kissing her mouth, her eyes.

"When I was a boy," he said, quickening his rhythm, breathing hard between the words, "I'd go swimming every morning. Off the rocks at Ayler's Point . . . it was beautiful. Cerulean water, palms. Chickens and pigs foraging. On the beach."

"Oh, God!" she said, locking her leg behind his thigh, her eyelids fluttering down.

"My first girlfriend was named Penny . . . she was twelve. Redheaded. I was a year younger. I loved her because she had freckles. I used to believe . . . freckles were . . . a sign of something. I wasn't sure what. But I love you more than her."

"I love you!" She found his rhythm, adapted to it, trying to take him all inside her. She wanted to see where they joined, and she imagined there was no longer any distinction between them, that their bodies had merged and were sealed together.

"I cheated in mathematics class, I could never do trigonometry. God . . . Catherine."

His voice receded, stopped, and the air seemed to grow solid around her, holding her in a rosy suspension. Light was gathering about them, frictive light from a strange heatless burning, and she heard herself crying out, calling his name, saying sweet things, childish things, telling him how wonderful he was, words like the words in a dream, important for their music, their sonority, rather than for any sense they made. She felt again the building of a dark wave in her belly. This time she flowed with it and let it carry her far.

Six

"Love's stupid," John said to her one day months later as they were sitting in the chamber of the heart, watching the complex eddying of golden light and whorls of shadow on the surface of the organ. "I feel like a damn sophomore. I keep finding myself thinking that I should do something noble. Feed the hungry, cure a disease." He made a noise of disgust. "It's as if I just woke up to the fact that the world has problems, and because I'm so happily in love, I want everyone else to be happy. But stuck . . . "

"Sometimes I feel like that myself," she said, startled by this outburst. "Maybe it's stupid, but it's not wrong. And neither is being happy."

"Stuck in here," he went on, "there's no

chance of doing anything for ourselves, let alone saving the world. As for being happy, that's not going to last . . . not in here, anyway."

"It's lasted six months," she said. "And if it won't last here, why should it last anywhere?"

He drew up his knees, rubbed the spot on his ankle where it had been fractured. "What's the matter with you? When I got here, all you could talk about was how much you wanted to escape. You said you'd do anything to get out. It sounds now that you don't care one way or the other."

She watched him rubbing the ankle, knowing what was coming. "I'd like very much to escape. Now that you're here, it's more acceptable to me. I can't deny that. That doesn't mean I wouldn't leave if I had the chance. But at least I can think about staying here without despairing."

"Well, I can't! I . . . " He lowered his head, suddenly drained of animation, still rubbing his ankle. "I'm sorry, Catherine. My leg's hurting again, and I'm in a foul mood." He cut his eyes toward her. "Have you got that stuff with you?"

"Yes."

She made no move to get it for him.

"I realize I'm taking too much," he said. "It helps pass the time."

She bristled at that and wanted to ask if she was the reason for his boredom; but she repressed her anger, knowing that she was partly to blame for his dependency on the brianine, that during his convalescence she had responded to his demands for the drug as a lover and not as a nurse.

An impatient look crossed his face. "Can I have it?"

Reluctantly she opened her pack, removed a flask of water and some pellets of brianine wrapped in cloth, and handed them over. He fumbled at the cloth, hurrying to unscrew the cap of the flask, and then — as he was about to swallow two of the pellets — he noticed her watching him. His face tightened with anger, and he appeared ready to snap at her. But his expression softened, and he downed the pellets, held out two more. "Take some with me," he said. "I know I have to stop. And I will. But let's just relax today, lets pretend we don't have any troubles . . . all right?"

That was a ploy he had adopted

recently, making her his accomplice in addiction and thus avoiding guilt; she knew she should refuse to join him, but at the moment she didn't have the strength for an argument. She took the pellets, washed them down with a swallow of water and lay back against the chamber wall. He settled beside her, leaning on one elbow, smiling, his eyes muddled-looking from the drug.

"You do have to stop, you know," she said.

His smile flickered, then steadied, as if his batteries were running low. "I suppose."

"If we're going to escape," she said, "you'll need a clear head."

He perked up at this. "That's a change."

"I haven't been thinking about escape for a long time. It didn't seem possible . . . it didn't even seem very important, anymore. I guess I'd given up on the idea. I mean just before you arrived, I'd been thinking about it again, but it wasn't serious . . . only frustration."

"And now?"

"It's become important again."

"Because of me, because I keep nagging about it?"

"Because of both of us. I'm not sure escape's possible, but I was wrong to stop trying."

He rolled onto his back, shielding his eyes with his forearm as if the heart's glow were too bright.

"John?" The name sounded thick and sluggish, and she could feel the drug taking her, making her drifty and slow.

"This place," he said. "This goddamn place."

"I thought," — she was beginning to have difficulty in ordering her words — "I thought you were excited by it. You used to talk . . . "

"Oh, I am excited!" He laughed dully. "It's a storehouse of marvels. Fantastic! Overwhelming! It's too overwhelming. The feeling here . . . " He turned to her. "Don't you feel it?"

"I'm not sure what you mean."

"How could you stand living here for all these years? Are you that much stronger than me, or are you just insensitive?"

"I'm . . . "

"God!"

He turned away, stared at the heart wall, his face tattooed with an convoluted flow of light and shadow, then flaring gold.

"You're so at ease here. Look at that."
He pointed to the heart. "It's not a heart,
it's a bloody act of magic. Every time I
come here I get the feeling it's going to
display a pattern that'll make me
disappear. Or crush me. Or something.
And you just sit there looking at it with a
thoughtful expression as if you're planning
to put in curtains or repaint the damned
thing."

"We don't have to come here
anymore."

"I can't stay away," he said, and held up
a pellet of brianine. "It's like this stuff."

They didn't speak for several
minutes . . . perhaps a bit less, perhaps a
little more. Time had become meaningless, and Catherine felt that she was
floating away, her flesh suffused with a
rosy warmth like the warmth of lovemak-
ing. Flashes of dream imagery passed
through her mind: a clown's monstrous
face; an unfamiliar room with tilted walls
and three-legged blue chairs; a painting
whose paint was melting, dripping.
The flashes lapsed into thoughts of John.
He was becoming weaker every day, she
realized. Losing his resilience, growing
nervous and moody. She had tried to

convince herself that sooner or later he would become adjusted to life inside Griaule, but she was beginning to accept the fact that he was not going to be able to survive here. She didn't understand why, whether it was due — as he had said — to the dragon's oppressiveness or to some inherent weakness. Or a combination of both. But she could no longer deny it, and the only option left was for them to effect an escape. It was easy to consider escape with the drug in her veins, feeling aloof and calm, possessed of a dreamlike overview; but she knew that once it wore off she would be at a loss as to how to proceed.

To avoid thinking, she let the heart's patterns dominate her attention. They seemed abnormally complex, and as she watched she began to have the impression of something new at work, some interior mechanism that she had never noticed before, and to become aware that the sense of imminence that pervaded the chamber was stronger than ever before; but she was so muzzy-headed that she could not concentrate upon these things. Her eyelids drooped, and she fell into her recurring dream of the sleeping dragon, focusing on the smooth scaleless skin of its chest, a patch of whiteness that came to surround her, to draw her into a world of whiteness with the serene constancy of its rhythmic rise and fall, as unvarying and predictable as the ticking of a perfect clock.

Over the next six months Catherine devised numerous plans for escape, but discarded them all as unworkable until at last she thought of one that — although far from foolproof — seemed in its simplicity to offer the least risk of failure. Though without brianine the plan would have failed, the process of settling upon this particular plan would have gone faster had drugs not been available; unable to resist the combined pull of the drug and John's need for companionship in his addiction, she herself had become an addict, and much of her time was spent lying at the heart with John, stupified, too enervated even to make love. Her feelings toward John had changed; it could not have been otherwise, for he was not the man he had been. He had lost weight and muscle tone, grown vague and brooding, and she was concerned for the health of his body and soul. In some ways she felt closer than ever to him, her maternal instincts having been engaged by his dissolution; yet she couldn't help resenting the fact that he had failed her, that instead of offering relief, he had turned out to be a burden and a weakening influence; and as a result whenever some distance arose between them, she exerted herself to close it only if it was practical to do so. This was not often the case, because John had deteriorated to the point that closeness of any sort was a chore. However, Catherine clung to the hope that if they could escape, they would be able to make a new beginning.

The drug owned her. She carried a supply of pellets wherever she went, gradually increasing her dosages, and not only did it affect her health, her energy, it had a profound effect upon her mind. Her powers of concentration were diminished, her sleep became fitful, and she began to experience hallucinations. She heard voices, strange noises, and on one occasion she was certain that she had spotted old Amos Mauldry among a group of Feelys milling about at the bottom of the colony chamber. Her mental erosion caused her to mistrust the information of her senses and to dismiss as delusion the intimations of some climactic event that came to her in dreams and from the patterns of light and shadow on the heart; and recognizing that certain of her symptoms — hearkening to inaudible signals and the like — were similar to the behavior of the Feelys, she feared that she was becoming one of them. Yet this fear was not so pronounced as once it might have been. She sought now to be tolerant of them, to overlook their role in her imprisonment, perceiving them as unwitting agents of Griaule, and she could not be satisfied in hating either them or the dragon; Griaule and the subtle manifestations of his will were something too vast and incomprehensible to be a target for hatred, and she transferred all her wrath to Brianne, the woman who had betrayed her. The Feelys seemed to notice this evolution in her attitude, and they became more familiar, attaching themselves to her wherever she went, asking questions, touching her, and while this made it difficult to achieve privacy, in the end it was their increased affection that inspired her plan.

One day, accompanied by a group of giggling, chattering Feelys, she walked up toward the skull, to the channel that led to the cavity containing the ghostvine. She ducked into the channel, half-tempted to explore the cavity again; but she decided against this course and on crawling out of the channel, she discovered that the Feelys had vanished. Suddenly weak, as if their presence had been an actual physical support, she sank to her knees and stared along the narrow passage of pale red flesh that wound away into a golden murk like a burrow leading to a shining treasure. She felt a welling up of petulant anger at the Feelys for having deserted her. Of course she should have expected it. They shunned this area like . . . She sat up, struck by a realization attendant to that thought. How far, she wondered, had the Feelys retreated? Could they have gone beyond the side passage that opened into the throat? She came to her feet and crept along the passage until she reached the curve. She peeked out around it, and seeing no one, continued on, holding her breath until her chest began to ache. She heard voices, peered around the next curve, and caught sight of eight Feelys gathered by the entrance to the side passage, their silken rags agleam, their swords reflecting glints of the inconstant light. She went back around the curve, rested against the wall; she had trouble thinking, in shaping thought into a coherent stream, and out of reflex she fumbled in her pack for some brianine. Just touching one of the pellets acted to calm her, and once she had swallowed it she breathed easier. She fixed her eyes on the blurred shape of a vein buried beneath the glistening ceiling of the passage, letting the fluctuations of light mesmerize her. She felt she was blurring, becoming golden and liquid and slow, and in that feeling she found a core of confidence and hope.

There's a way, she told herself; *My God, maybe there really is a way.*

By the time she had fleshed out her plan three days later, her chief fear was that John wouldn't be able to function well enough to take part in it. He looked awful, his cheeks sunken, his color poor, and the first time she tried to tell him about the plan, he fell asleep. To counteract the brianine she began cutting his dosage, mixing it with the stimulant she had derived from the lichen growing on the dragon's lung, and after a few days, though his color and general appearance did not improve, he became more alert and energized. She knew the improvement was purely chemical, that the stimulant was a danger in his weakened state; but there was no alternative, and this at least offered him a chance at life. If he were to remain there, given the physical erosion caused by the drug, she did not believe he would last another six months.

It wasn't much of a plan, nothing subtle, nothing complex, and if she'd had her wits about her, she thought, she would have come up with it long before; but she doubted she would have had the courage to try it alone, and if there was trouble, then two people wound stand a much better chance than one. John was elated by the prospect. After she had told him the particulars he paced up and down in their bedroom, his eyes bright, hectic spots of red dappling his cheeks, stopping now and again to question her or to make distracted comments.

"The Feelys," he said. "We . . . uh . . . we

won't hurt them?"

"I told you . . . not unless it's necessary."

"That's good, that's good." He crossed the room to the curtains drawn across the entrance. "Of course it's not my field, but . . ."

"John?"

He peered out at the colony through the gap in the curtains, the skin on his forehead washing from gold to dark. "Uh-huh."

"What's not your field?"

After a long pause he said, "It's not . . . nothing."

"You were talking about the Feelys."

"They're very interesting," he said distractedly. He swayed, then moved sluggishly toward her, collapsed on the pile of furs where she was sitting. He turned his face to her, looked at her with a morose expression. "It'll be better," he said. "Once we're out of here, I'll . . . I know I haven't been . . . strong. I haven't been . . . "

"It's all right," she said, stroking his hair.

"No, it's not, it's not." Agitated, he struggled to sit up, but she restrained him, telling him not to be upset, and soon he lay still. "How can you love me?" he asked after a long silence.

"I don't have any choice in the matter." She bent to him, pushing back her hair so it wouldn't hang in his face, kissed his cheek, his eyes.

He started to say something, then laughed weakly, and she asked him what he found amusing.

"I was thinking about free will," he said. "How improbable a concept that's become. Here. Where it's so obviously not an option."

She settled down beside him, weary of trying to boost his spirits. She remembered how he'd been after his arrival: eager, alive, and full of curiosity despite his injuries. Now his moments of greatest vitality — like this one — were spent in sardonic rejection of happy possibility. She was tired of arguing with him, of making the point that everything in life could be reduced by negative logic to a sort of pitiful reflex, if that was the way you wanted to see it. His voice grew stronger, this prompted — she knew — by a rush of the stimulant within his system.

"It's Griaule," he said. "Everything here belongs to him, even to the most fleeting of hopes and wishes. What we feel, what we think. When I was a student and first heard about Griaule, about his method of dominion, the omnipotent functioning of his will, I thought it was foolishness pure and simple. But I was an optimist, then. And optimists are only fools without experience. Of course I didn't think of myself as an optimist. I saw myself as a realist. I had a romantic notion that I was alone, responsible for my actions, and I perceived that as being a noble beauty, a refinement of the tragic . . . that state of utter and forlorn independence. I thought how cozy and unrealistic it was for people to depend on gods and demons to define their roles in life. I didn't know how terrible it would be to realize that nothing you thought or did had any individual importance, that everything — love, hate, your petty likes and dislikes — was part of some unfathomable scheme. I couldn't comprehend how worthless that knowledge would make you feel."

He went on in this vein for some time, his words weighing on her, filling her with despair, pushing hope aside. Then, as if this monologue had aroused some bitter sexuality, he began to make love to her. She felt removed from the act, imprisoned within walls erected by his dour sentences; but she responded with desperate enthusiasm, her own arousal funded by a desolate prurience. She watched his spread-fingered hands knead and cup her breasts, actions that seemed to her as devoid of emotional value as those of a starfish gripping a rock; and yet because of this desolation, because she wanted to deny it and also because of the voyeuristic thrill she derived from watching herself being taken, used, her body reacted with unusual fervor. The sweaty film between them was like a silken cloth, and their movements seemed more accomplished and supple than ever before; each jolt of pleasure brought her to new and dizzying heights. But afterward she felt devastated and defeated, not loved, and lying there with him, listening to the muted gabble of the Feelys from without, bathed in their rich stench, she knew she had come to the nadir of her life, that she had finally united with the Feelys in their enactment of a perturbed and animalistic rhythm.

Over the next ten days she set the plan into motion. She took to dispensing little sweet cakes to the Feelys who guarded her on her daily walks with John, ending up each time at the channel that led to the ghostvine. And she also began to spread the rumor that at long last her study of the dragon was about to yield its promised revelation. On the day of the escape, prior to going forth, she stood at the bottom of the chamber, surrounded by hundreds of Feelys, more hanging on ropes just above her, and called out to them in ringing tones, "Today I will have word for you! Griaule's word! Bring together the hunters and those who gather food, and have them wait here for me! I will return soon, very soon, and speak to you of what is to come!"

The Feelys jostled and pawed one another, chattering, tittering, hopping up and down, and some of those hanging from the ropes were so overcome with excitement that they lost their grip and fell, landing atop their fellows, creating squirming heaps of Feelys who squalled and yelped and then started fumbling with the buttons of each other's clothing. Catherine waved at them, and with John at her side, set out toward the cavity, six Feelys with swords at their rear.

John was terribly nervous and all during the walk he kept casting backward glances at the Feelys, asking questions that only served to unnerve Catherine. "Are you sure they'll eat them?" he said. "Maybe they won't be hungry."

"They always eat them while we're in the channel," she said. "You know that."

"I know," he said. "But I'm just . . . I don't want anything to go wrong." He walked another half-a dozen paces. "Are you sure you put enough in the cakes?"

"I'm sure." She watched him out of the corner of her eye. The muscles in his jaw bunched, nerves twitched in his cheek. A light sweat had broken on his forehead, and his pallor was extreme. She took his arm. "How do you feel?"

"Fine," he said. "I'm fine."

"Its going to work, so don't worry . . . please."

"I'm fine," he repeated, his voice dead, eyes fixed straight ahead.

The Feelys came to a halt just around the curve from the channel, and Catherine, smiling at them, handed them each a cake; then she and John went forward and crawled into the channel. There they sat in the darkness without speaking, their hips touching. At last John whispered, "How much longer?"

"Let's give it a few more minutes . . . just to be safe."

He shuddered, and she asked again how he felt.

"A little shaky," he said. "But I'm all right."

She put her hand on his arm; his muscles jumped at the touch. "Calm down," she said, and he nodded. But there was no slackening of his tension.

The seconds passed with the slowness of sap welling from cut bark, and despite her certainty that all would go as planned, Catherine's anxiety increased. Little shiny squiggles, velvety darknesses blacker than the air, wormed in front of her eyes. She imagined that she heard whispers out in the passage. She tried to think of something else, but the concerns she erected to occupy her mind materialized and vanished with a superficial and formal precision that did nothing to ease her, seeming mere transparencies shunted across the vision of a fearful prospect ahead. Finally she gave John a nudge and they crept from the channel, made their way cautiously along the passage. When they reached the curve beyond which the Feelys were waiting, she paused, listened.

Not a sound. She looked out. Six bodies lay by the entrance to the side passage; even at that distance she could spot the half-eaten cakes that had fallen from their hands. Still wary, they approached the Feelys, and as they came near, Catherine thought that there was something unnatural about their stillness. She knelt beside a young male, caught a whiff of loosened bowl, saw the rapt character of death stamped on his features and realized that in measuring out the dosages of brianine in each cake, she had not taken the Feelys' slightness of build into account. She had killed them.

"Come on!" said John. He had picked up two swords; they were so short, they looked toylike in his hands. He handed over one of the swords and helped her to stand. "Let's go . . . there might be more of them!"

He wetted his lips, glanced from side to side. With his sunken cheeks and hollowed eyes, his face had the appearance of a skull, and for a moment, dumbstruck by the realization that she had killed, by the understanding that for all her disparagement of them, the Feelys were human, Catherine failed to recognize him. She stared at them — like ugly dolls in the ruins of their gaud — and felt again that same chill emptiness that had possessed her when she had killed Key Willen. John caught her arm, pushed her toward the side passage; it was covered by a loose flap, and though she had become used to seeing the dragon's flesh everywhere, she now shrank from touching it. John pulled back the flap, urged her into the passage, and then they were crawling through a golden gloom, following a twisting downward course.

In places the passage was only a few inches wider than her hips, and they were forced to worm their way along. She imagined that she could feel the immense weight of the dragon pressing in upon her, pictured some muscle twitching in reflex, the passage constricting and crushing them. The closed space made her breathing sound loud, and for awhile John's breathing sounded even louder, hoarse and labored. But then she could no longer hear it, and she discovered that he had fallen behind. She called out to him, and he said, "Keep going!"

She rolled onto her back in order to see him. He was gasping, his face twisted as if in pain. "What's wrong?" she cried, trying to turn completely, constrained from doing so by the narrowness of the passage.

He gave her a shove. "I'll be all right. Don't stop!"

"John!" She stretched out a hand to him, and he wedged his shoulder against her legs, pushing her along.

"Damn it . . . just keep going!" He continued to push and exhort her, and realizing that she could do nothing, she turned and crawled at an even faster pace, seeing his harrowed face in her mind's eye.

She couldn't tell how many minutes it took to reach the end of the passage; it was a timeless time, one long unfractionated moment of straining, squirming, pulling at the slick walls, her effort fueled by her concern; but when she scrambled out into the dragon's throat, her heart racing, for an instant she forgot about John, about everything except the sight before her. From where she stood the throat sloped upward and widened into the mouth, and through that great opening came a golden light, not the heavy mineral brilliance of Griaule's blood, but a fresh clear light, penetrating the

tangled shapes of the thickets in beams
made crystalline by dust and moisture —
the light of day. The tip of a huge fang
hooking upward, stained gold with the
morning sun, and the vault of the dragon's
mouth above, with its vines and epiphytes.
Stunned, gaping, she dropped her sword
and went a couple of paces toward the
light. It was so clean, so pure, its allure like
a call. Remembering John, she turned
back to the passage. He was pushing
himself erect with his sword, his face
flushed, panting.

"Look!" she said, hurrying to him,
pointing at the light. "God, just look at
that!" She steadied him, began steering
him toward the mouth.

"We made it," he said. "I didn't believe
we would."

His hand tightened on her arm in what
she assumed was a sign of affection;
but then his grip tightened cruelly, and he
lurched backward.

"John!" She fought to hold onto him,
saw that his eyes had rolled up into his
head.

He sprawled onto his back, and she
went down on her knees beside him,
hands fluttering above his chest, saying,

"John? John?" What felt like a shiver passed through his body, a faint guttering noise issued from his throat, and she knew, oh, she knew very well the meaning of that tremor, that signal passage of breath. She drew back, confused, staring at his face. certain that she had gotten things wrong, that in a second or two his eyelids would open. But they did not. "John?" she said, astonished by how calm she felt, by the measured tone of her voice, as if she were making a simple inquiry. She wanted to break through the shell of calmness, to let out what she was really feeling, but it was as if some strangely lucid twin had gained control over her muscles and will. Her face was cold, and she got to her feet, thinking that the coldness must be radiating from John's body and that distance would be a cure. The sight of him lying there frightened her, and she turned her back on him, folded her arms across her chest. She blinked against the daylight. It hurt her eyes, and the loops and interlacings of foliage standing out in silhouette also hurt her with their messy complexity, their disorder. She couldn't decide what to do. Get away, she told herself. Get out. She took a hesitant step toward the mouth, but that direction didn't make sense. No direction made sense, anymore.

Something moved in the bushes, but she paid it no mind. Her calm was beginning to crack, and a powerful gravity seemed to be pulling her back toward the body. She tried to resist it. More movement. Leaves were rustling, branches being pushed aside. Lots of little movements. She wiped at her eyes. There were no tears in them, but something was hampering her vision, something opaque and thin, a tattered film. The shreds of her calm, she thought, and laughed . . . more a hiccup than a laugh. She managed to focus on the bushes and saw ten, twenty, no, more, maybe two or three dozen diminutive figures, pale mongrel children in glittering rags standing at the verge of the thicket. She hiccuped again, and this time it felt nothing like a laugh. A sob, or maybe nausea. The Feelys shifted nearer, edging toward her. The bastards had been waiting for them. She and John had never had a chance of escaping.

Catherine retreated to the body, reached down, groping for John's sword. She picked it up, pointed it at them. "Stay away from me," she said. "Just stay away, and I won't hurt you."

They came closer, shuffling, their shoulders hunched, their attitudes fearful, but advancing steadily all the same.

"Stay away!" she shouted. "I swear I'll kill you!" She swung the sword, making a windy arc through the air. "I swear!"

The Feelys gave no sign of having heard, continuing their advance, and Catherine, sobbing now, shrieked for them to keep back, swinging the sword again and again. They encircled her, standing just beyond range. "You don't believe me?" she said. "You don't believe I'll kill you? I don't have any reason not to." All her grief and fury broke through, and with a scream she lunged at the Feelys, stabbing one in the stomach, slicing a line of blood across the satin and gilt chest of another. The two she had wounded fell, shrilling their agony, and the rest swarmed toward her. She split the skull of another, split it as easily as she might have a melon, saw gore and splintered bone fly from the terrible wound, the dead male's face nearly halved, more blood leaking from around his eyes as he toppled, and then the rest of them were on her, pulling her

down, pummeling her, giving little fey cries.
She had no chance against them, but she
kept on fighting, knowing that when
she stopped, when she surrendered, she
would have to start feeling, and that
she wanted badly to avoid. Their vapid
faces hovered above her, seeming
uniformly puzzled, as if unable to
understand her behavior, and the mild-
ness of their reactions infuriated her.
Death should have brightened them,
made them — like her — hot with rage.
Screaming again, her thoughts reddening,
pumped with adrenaline, she struggled to
her knees, trying to shake off the Feelys
who clung to her arms. Snapping her
teeth at fingers, faces, arms. Then
something struck the back of her head,
and she sagged, her vision whirling,
darkness closing in until all she could see
was a tunnel of shadow with someone's
watery eyes at the far end. The eyes grew
wider, merged into a single eye that was
itself a shadow with leathery wings and a
forked tongue and a belly full of fire that
swooped down, open-mouthed, to swallow her up and fly her home.

Seven

The drug moderated Catherine's grief ... or perhaps it was more than the drug. John's decline had begun so soon after they had met, it seemed she had become accustomed to sadness in relation to him, and thus his death had not overwhelmed her, but rather had manifested as an ache in her chest and a heaviness in her limbs, like small stones she was forced to carry about. To rid of herself of that ache, that heaviness, she increased her use of the drug, eating the pellets as if they were candy, gradually withdrawing from life. She had no use for life any longer. She knew she was going to die within the dragon, knew it with the same clarity and certainty that accompanied all Griaule's sendings — death was to be her punishment for seeking to avoid his will, for denying his right to define and delimit her.

After the escape attempt, the Feelys had treated her with suspicion and hostility; recently they had been absorbed by some internal matter, agitated in the extreme, and they had taken to ignoring her. Without their minimal companion-ship, without John, the patterns flowing across the surface of the heart were the only thing that took Catherine out of herself, and she spent hours at a time watching them, lying there half-conscious, registering their changes through slitted eyes. As her addiction worsened, as she lost weight and muscle tone, she became even more expert in interpreting the patterns, and staring up at the vast curve of the heart, like the curve of a golden bell, she came to realize that Mauldry had been right, that the dragon was a god, a universe unto itself with its own laws and physical constants. A god that she hated. She would try to beam her hatred at the heart, hoping to cause a rupture, a seizure of some sort; but she knew that Griaule was impervious to this, impervious to all human weapons, and that her hatred would have as little effect upon him as an arrow loosed into an empty sky.

One day almost a year after John's death she waked abruptly from a dreamless sleep beside the heart, sitting bolt upright, feeling that a cold spike had been driven down the hollow of her spine. She rubbed sleep from her eyes, trying to shake off the lethargy of the drug, sensing danger at hand. Then she glanced up at the heart and was struck motionless. The patterns of shadow and golden radiance were changing more rapidly than ever before, and their complexity, too, was far greater than she had ever seen; yet they were as clear to her as her own script: pulsings of darkness and golden eddies flowing, unscrolling across the dimpled surface of the organ. It was a simple message, and for a few seconds she refused to accept the knowledge it conveyed, not wanting to believe that this was the culmination of her destiny, that her youth had been wasted in so trivial a matter; but recalling all the clues, the dreams of the sleeping dragon, the repetitious vision of the rise and fall of its chest, Mauldry's story of the first Feely, the exodus of animals and insects and birds,

the muffled thud from deep within the
dragon after which everything had remained calm for a thousand years . . . she
knew it must be true.

As it had done a thousand years
before, and as it would do again a thous-
and years in the future, the heart was
going to beat.

She was infuriated, and she wanted to
reject the fact that all her trials and griefs
had been sacrifices made for the sole
purpose of saving the Feelys. Her task,
she realized, would be to clear them out of
the chamber where they lived before it
was flooded with the liquids that fueled
the dragon's fires; and after the chamber
had been emptied, she was to lead them
back so they could go on with the work of
keeping Griaule pest-free. The cause of
their recent agitation, she thought, must
have been due to their apprehension of
the event, the result of one of Griaule's
sendings; but because of their temerity
they would tend to dismiss his warning,
being more frightened of the outside
world than of any peril within the dragon.
They would need guidance to survive, and
as once he had chose Mauldry to assist
her, now Griaule had chosen her to guide

the Feelys.

She staggered up, as befuddled as a bird trapped between glass walls, making little rushes this way and that; then anger overcame confusion, and she beat with her fists on the heart wall, bawling her hatred of the dragon, her anguish at the ruin he had made of her life. Finally, breathless, she collapsed, her own heart pounding erratically, trying to think what to do. She wouldn't tell them, she decided; she would just let them die when the chamber flooded, and this way have her revenge. But an instant later she reversed her decision, knowing that the Feelys' deaths would merely be an inconvenience to Griaule, that he would simply gather a new group of idiots to serve him. And besides, she thought, she had already killed too many Feelys. There was no choice, she realized; over the span of almost eleven years she had been maneuvered by the dragon's will to this place and moment where, by virtue of her shaped history and conscience, she had only one course of action.

Full of muddle-headed good intentions, she made her way back to the colony, her guards trailing behind, and

when she had reached the chamber,
she stood with her back to the channel
that led toward the throat, uncertain of
how to proceed. Several hundred Feelys
were milling about the bottom of the
chamber, and others were clinging to
ropes, hanging together in front of one or
another of the cubicles, looking in that
immense space like clusters of glittering,
many-colored fruit; the constant motion
and complexity of the colony added to
Catherine's hesitancy and bewilderment,
and when she tried to call out to the
Feelys, to gain their attention, she
managed only a feeble, scratchy noise.
But she gathered her strength and called
out again and again, until at last they were
all assembled before her, silent and
staring, hemming her in against the
entrance to the channel, next to some
chests that contained the torches and
swords and other items used by the
hunters. The Feelys gaped at her, plucking
at their gaudy rags; their silence seemed to
have a slow vibration. Catherine started
to speak, but faltered; she took a deep
breath, let it out explosively and made a
second try.

"We have to leave," she said, hearing

the shakiness of her voice. "We have to go outside. Not for long. Just for a little while . . . a few hours. The chamber, it's going . . . " She broke off, realizing that they weren't following her. "The thing Griaule has meant me to learn," she went on in a louder voice, "at last I know it. I know why I was brought to you. I know the purpose for which I have studied all these years. Griaule's heart is going to beat, and when it does the chamber will fill with liquid. If you remain here, you'll all drown."

The front ranks shifted, and some of the Feelys exchanged glances, but otherwise they displayed no reaction.

Catherine shook her fists in frustration. "You'll die if you don't listen to me! You have to leave! When the heart contracts, the chamber will be flooded . . . don't you understand?" She pointed up to the mist-hung ceiling of the chamber. "Look! The birds . . . the birds have gone! They know what's coming! And so do you! Don't you feel the danger? I know you do!"

They edged back, some of them turning away, entering into whispered exchanges with their fellows.

Catherine grabbed the nearest of them,

a young female dressed in ruby silks. "Listen to me!" she shouted.

"Liar, Cat'rine, liar," said one of the males, jerking the female away from her. "We not goin' be mo' fools."

"I'm not lying! I'm not!" She went from one to another, putting her hands on their shoulders, meeting their eyes in an attempt to impress them with her sincerity. "The heart is going to beat! Once . . . just once. You won't have to stay outside long. Not long at all."

They were all walking away, all beginning to involve themselves in their own affairs, and Catherine, desperate, hurried after them, pulling them back, saying, "Listen to me! Please!" Explaining what was to happen, and receiving cold stares in return. One of the males shoved her aside, baring his teeth in a hiss, his eyes blank and bright, and she retreated to the entrance of the channel, feeling rattled and disoriented, in need of another pellet. She couldn't collect her thoughts, and she looked around in every direction as if hoping to find some sight that would steady her; but nothing she saw was of any help. Then her gaze settled on the chests where the swords and torches were stored. She felt as if her head were being held in a vise and forced toward the chests, and the knowledge of what she must do was a coldness inside her head — the unmistakable touch of Griaule's thought. It was the only way. She saw that clearly. But the idea of doing something so extreme frightened her, and she hesitated, looking behind her to make sure that none of the Feelys were keeping track of her movements. She inched toward the chests, keeping her eyes lowered, trying to make it appear that she was moving aimlessly. In one of the chests were a number of tinderboxes resting beside some torches; she stooped, grabbed a torch and one of the tinderboxes, and went walking briskly up the slope. She paused by the lowest rank of cubicles, noticed that some of the Feelys had turned to watch her; when she lit the torch, alarm surfaced in their faces and they surged up the slope toward her. She held the torch up to the curtains that covered the entrance to the cubicle, and the Feelys fell back, muttering, some letting out piercing wails.

"Please!" Catherine cried, her knees rubbery from the tension, a chill knot in her breast. "I don't want to do this! But you have to leave!"

A few of the Feelys edged toward the channel, and encouraged by this, Catherine shouted, "Yes! That's it! If you'll just go outside, just for a little while, I won't have to do it!"

Several Feelys entered the channel, and the crowd around Catherine began to erode, whimpering, breaking into tears, trickles of five and six at a time breaking away and moving out of sight within the channel, until there were no more than thirty of them left within the chamber, forming a ragged semi-circle around her. She would have liked to believe that they would do as she had suggested without further coercion on her part, but she knew that they were all packed into the channel or the chamber beyond, waiting for her to put down the torch. She gestured at the Feelys surrounding her, and they, too, began easing toward the channel; when only a handful of them remained visible, she touched the torch to the curtains.

She was amazed by how quickly the fire spread, rushing like waves up the silk drapes, following the rickety outlines of the cubicles, appearing to dress them in a fancywork of reddish yellow flame, making crispy, chuckling noises. The fire seemed to have a will of its own, to be playfully seeking out all the intricate shapes of the colony and illuminating them, the separate flames chasing one another with merry abandon, sending little trains of fire along poles and stanchions, geysering up from corners, flinging out fiery fingers to touch tips across a gap.

She was so caught up in this display, her drugged mind finding in it an aesthetic, that she forgot all about the Feelys, and when a cold sharp pain penetrated her left side, she associated this not with them but thought it a side-effect of the drug, a sudden attack brought on by her abuse of it. Then, horribly weak, sinking to her knees, she saw one of them standing next to her, a male with a pale thatch of thinning hair wisping across his scalp, holding a sword tipped with red, and she knew that he had stabbed her. She had the giddy urge to speak to him, not out of anger, just to ask a question that she wasn't able to speak, for instead of being afraid of the weakness invading her limbs, she had a terrific curiosity about what would happen next, and she had the irrational thought that her executioner might have the answer, that in his role as the instrument of Griaule's will he might have some knowledge of absolutes. He spat something at her, an accusation or an insult made inaudible by the crackling of the flames, and fled down the slope and out of the chamber, leaving her alone. She rolled onto her back, gazing at the fire, and the pain seemed to roll inside her as if it were a separate thing. Some of the cubicles were collapsing, spraying sparks, twists of black smoke boiling up, smouldering pieces of blackened wood tumbling down to the chamber floor, the entire structure appearing to ripple through the heat haze, looking unreal, an absurd construction of flaming skeletal framework and billowing, burning silks, and growing dizzy, feeling that she was falling upward into that huge fiery space, Catherine passed out.

She must have been unconscious for only a matter of seconds, because nothing had changed when she opened her eyes, except that a section of the fabric covering the chamber floor had caught fire. The flames were roaring, the snaps of cracking timber as sharp as explosions, and her nostrils were choked with an acrid stink. With a tremendous effort that brought her once again to the edge of unconsciousness, she came to her feet, clutching the wound in her side, and stumbled toward the channel; at the entrance she fell and crawled into it, choking on the smoke that poured along the passageway. Her eyes teared from the smoke, and she wriggled on her stomach, pulling herself along with her hands. She nearly passed out a half dozen times before reaching the adjoining chamber, and then she staggered, crawled, stopping frequently to catch her breath, to let the pain of her wound subside, somehow negotiating a circuitous path among the pools of burning liquid and the pale red warty bumps that sprouted everywhere. Then into the throat. She wanted to surrender to the darkness there, to let go, but she kept going, not motivated by fear, but by some reflex of survival, simply obeying the impulse to continue for as long as it was possible. Her eyes blurred, and darkness frittered at the edges of her vision. But even so, she was able to make out the light of day, the menagerie of shapes erected by the interlocking branches of the thickets, and she thought that now she could stop, that this had been what she wanted — to see the light again, not to die bathed in the uncanny radiance of Griaule's blood.

She lay down, lowering herself cautiously among a bed of ferns, her back against the side of the throat, the same position — she remembered — in which she had fallen asleep that first night inside the dragon so many years before. She started to slip, to dwindle inside herself, but was alerted by a whispery rustling that grew louder and louder, and a moment later swarms of insects began to pour from the dragon's throat, passing overhead with a whirring rush and in such density that they cut off most of the light issuing from the mouth. Far above, like the shadows of spiders, apes were swinging on the vines that depended from the roof of the mouth, heading for the outer world, and Catherine could hear smaller animals scuttling through the brush. The sight of these flights made her feel accomplished, secure in what she had done, and she settled back, resting her head against Griaule's flesh, as peaceful as she could ever recall, almost eager to be done with life, with drugs and solitude and violence. She had a moment's worry about the Feelys, wondering where they were; but then she realized that they would probably do no differently than had their remote ancestor, that they would hide in the thickets until all was calm.

She let her eyes close. The pain of the wound had diminished to a distant throb that scarcely troubled her, and the throbbing made a rhythm that seemed to be bearing her up. Somebody was talking to her, saying her name, and she resisted the urge to open her eyes, not wanting to be called back. She must be hearing things, she thought. But the voice persisted, and at last she did open her eyes. She gave a weak laugh on seeing Amos Mauldry kneeling before her, wavering and vague as a ghost, and realized that she was seeing things, too.

"Catherine," he said. "Can you hear me?"

"No," she said, and laughed again, a laugh that sent her into a bout of gasping; she felt her weakness in a new and poignant way, and it frightened her.

"Catherine?"

She blinked, trying to make him disappear; but he appeared to solidify as if she were becoming more part of his world than that of life. "What is it, Mauldry?" she said, and coughed. "Have you come to guide me to heaven . . . is that it?"

His lips moved, and she had the idea that he was trying to reassure her of something; but she couldn't hear his words, no matter how hard she strained her ears. He was beginning to fade, becoming opaque, proving himself to be no more than a phantom; yet as she blacked out, experiencing a final moment of panic, Catherine could have sworn that she felt him take her hand.

She awoke in a golden glow that dimmed and brightened, and found herself staring into a face; after a moment, a long moment, because the face was much different than she had imagined it during these past few years, she recognized that it was hers. She lay still, trying to accommodate to this state of affairs, wondering why she wasn't dead, puzzling over the face and uncertain why she wasn't afraid; she felt strong and alert and at peace. She sat up and discovered that she was naked, that she was sitting in a small chamber lit by veins of golden blood branching across the ceiling, its walls obscured by vines with glossy dark green leaves. The body — her body — was lying on its back, and one side of the shirt it wore was soaked with blood. Folded beside the body was a fresh shirt, trousers, and resting atop these was a pair of sandals.

She checked her side — there was no sign of a wound. Her emotions were a mix of relief and self-loathing. She understood that somehow she had been conveyed to this cavity, to the ghostvine, and her essences had been transferred to a likeness, and yet she had trouble accepting the fact, because she felt no different than she had before . . . except for the feelings of peace and strength, and the fact that she had no craving for the drug. She tried to deny what had happened, to deny that she was now a thing, the bizarre contrivance of a plant, and it seemed that her thoughts, familiar in their ordinary process, were proofs that she must be wrong in her assumption. However, the body was an even more powerful evidence to the contrary. She would have liked to take refuge in panic, but her overall feeling of well-being prevented this. She began to grow cold, her skin pebbling, and reluctantly she dressed in the clothing folded beside the body. Something hard in the breast pocket of the shirt. She opened the pocket, took out a small leather sack; she loosed the tie of the sack and from it poured a fortune of cut gems into her hand: diamonds, emeralds, and sunstones. She put the sack back into the pocket, not knowing what to make of the stones, and sat looking at the body. It was much changed from its youth, leaner, less voluptuous, and in the repose of death, the face had lost its gloss and perfection, and was merely the face of an attractive woman . . . a disheartened woman. She thought she should feel something, that she should be oppressed by the sight, but she had no reaction to it; it might have been a skin she had shed, something of no more consequence than that.

She had no idea where to go, but realizing that she couldn't stay there forever, she stood and with a last glance at the body, she made her way down the narrow channel leading away from the cavity. When she emerged into the passage, she hesitated, unsure of which direction to choose, unsure, too, of which direction was open to her. At length, deciding not to tempt Griaule's judgment, she headed back toward the colony, thinking that she would take part in helping them rebuild; but before she had gone ten feet she heard Mauldry's voice calling her name.

He was standing by the entrance to the cavity, dressed as he had been that first night — in a satin frock coat, carrying his gold-knobbed cane — and as she approached him, a smile broke across his wrinkled face, and he nodded as if in approval of her resurrection. "Surprised to see me?" he asked.

"I . . . I don't know," she said, a little afraid of him. "Was that you . . . in the mouth?"

He favored her with a polite bow. "None other. After things settled down, I had some of the Feelys bear you to the cavity. Or rather I was the one who effected Griaule's will in the matter. Did you look in the pocket of your shirt?"

"Yes."

"Then you found the gems. Good, good."

She was at a loss for words at first.

"I thought I saw you once before," she said finally. "A few years back."

"I'm sure you did. After my rebirth," — he gestured toward the cavity — "I was no longer of any use to you. You were forging your own path and my presence would have hampered your process. So I hid among the Feelys, waiting for the time when you would need me." He squinted at her. "You look troubled."

"I don't understand any of this," she said. "How can I feel like my old self, when I'm obviously so different?"

"Are you?" he asked. "Isn't sameness or difference mostly a matter of feeling?" He took her arm, steered her along the passage away from the colony. "You'll adjust to it, Catherine. I have, and I had the same reaction as you when I first awoke." He spread his arms, inviting her to examine him. "Do I look different to you? Aren't I the same old fool as ever?"

"So it seems," she said drily. She walked a few paces in silence, then something occurred to her. "The Feelys . . . do they . . . "

"Rebirth is only for the chosen, the select. The Feelys receive another sort of reward, one not given me to understand."

"You call this a reward? To be subject to more of Griaule's whims? And what's next for me? Am I to discover when his bowels are due to move?"

He stopped walking, frowning at her. "Next? Why, whatever pleases you, Catherine. I've been assuming that you'd want to leave, but you're free to do as you wish. Those gems I gave you will buy you any kind of life you desire."

"I can leave?"

"Most assuredly. You've accomplished your purpose here, and you're your own agent now. *Do* you want to leave?"

Catherine looked at him, unable to speak, and nodded.

"Well, then." He took her arm again. "Let's be off."

As they walked down to the chamber behind the throat and then into the throat itself, Catherine felt as one is supposed to feel at the moment of death, all the memories of her life within the dragon passing before her eyes with their attendant emotions — her flight, her labors and studies, John, the long hours spent beside the heart — and she thought that this was most appropriate, because she was not re-entering life but rather passing through into a kind of afterlife, a place beyond death that would be as unfamiliar and new a place as Griaule himself had once seemed. And she was astounded to realize that she was frightened of these new possibilities, that the thing she had wanted for so long could pose a menace and that it was the dragon who now offered the prospect of security. On several occasions she considered turning back, but each time she did, she rebuked herself for her timidity and continued on. However, on reaching the mouth and wending her way through the thickets, her fear grew more pronounced. The sunlight, that same light that not so many months before had been alluring, now hurt her eyes and made her want to draw back into the dim golden murk of Griaule's blood; and as they neared the lip, as she stepped into the shadow of a fang, she began to tremble with cold and stopped, hugging herself to keep warm.

Mauldry took up a position facing her, jogged her arm. "What is it?" he asked. "You seem frightened."

"I am," she said; she glanced up at him. "Maybe . . ."

"Don't be silly," he said. "You'll be fine

once you're away from here. And," — he cocked his eye toward the declining sun — "you should be pushing along. You don't want to be hanging about the mouth when it's dark. I doubt anything would harm you, but since you're no longer part of Griaule's plan . . . well, better safe than sorry." He gave her a push. "Get along with you, now."

"You're not coming with me?"

"Me?" Mauldry chuckled. "What would I do out there? I'm an old man, set in my ways. No, I'm far better off staying with the Feelys. I've become half a Feely myself after all these years. But you're young, you've got a whole world of life ahead of you." He nudged her forward. "Do what I say, girl. There's no use in your hanging about any longer."

She went a couple of steps toward the lip, paused, feeling sentimental about leaving the old man; though they had never been close, he had been like a father to her . . . and thinking this, remembering her real father, whom she had scarcely thought of these last years, with whom she'd had the same lack of closeness, that made her aware of all the things she had to look forward to, all the lost things she might now regain. She moved into the thickets with a firmer step, and behind her, old Mauldry called to her for a last time.

"That's my girl!" he sang out. "You just keep going, and you'll start to feel at rights soon enough! There's nothing to be afraid of . . . nothing you can avoid, in any case! Goodbye, goodbye!"

She glanced back, waved, saw him shaking his cane in a gesture of farewell, and laughed at his eccentric appearance: a funny little man in satin rags hopping up and down in that great shadow between the fangs. Out from beneath that shadow herself, the rich light warmed her, seeming to penetrate and dissolve all the coldness that had been lodged in her bones and thoughts.

"Goodbye!" cried Mauldry. "Goodbye! Don't be sad! You're not leaving anything important behind, and you're taking the best parts with you. Just walk fast and think about what you're going to tell everyone. They'll be amazed by all you've done! Flabbergasted! Tell them about Griaule! Tell them what he's like, tell them all you've seen and all you've learned. Tell them what a grand adventure you've had!"

Eight

Returning to Hangtown was in some ways a more unsettling experience than had been Catherine's flight into the dragon. She had expected the place to have changed, and while there *had* been minor changes, she had assumed that it would be as different from its old self as was she. But standing at the edge of the village, looking out at the gray weathered shacks ringing the fouled shallows of the lake, thin smokes issuing from tin chimneys, the cliff of the fronto-parietal plate casting its gloomy shadow, the chokecherry thickets, the hawthornes, the dark brown dirt of the streets, three elderly men sitting on cane chairs in front of one of the shacks, smoking their pipes and staring back at her with unabashed curiosity . . . superficially it was no different than it had been ten years before, and this seemed to imply that her years of imprisonment, her death and rebirth had been of small importance. She did not demand that they be important to anyone else, yet it galled her that the world had passed through those years of ordeal without significant scars, and it also imbued her with the irrational fear that if she were to enter the village, she might suffer some magical slippage back through time and re-inhabit her old life. At last, with a hesitant step, she walked over to the men and wished them a good morning.

"Mornin'," said a paunchy fellow with a mottled bald scalp and a fringe of gray beard, whom she recognized as Tim Weedlon. "What can I do for you, ma'am? Got some nice bits of scale inside."

"That place over there," — she pointed to an abandoned shack down the street, its roof holed and missing the door — "where can I find the owner?"

The other man, Mardo Koren, thin as a mantis, his face seamed and blotched, said, "Can't nobody say for sure. Ol' Riall died . . . must be goin' on nine, ten years back."

"He's dead?"   She felt weak inside, dazed.

"Yep," said Tim Weedlon, studying her face, his brow furrowed, his expression bewildered. "His daughter run away, killed a village man name of Willen and vanished into nowhere . . . or so ever'body figured.   Then when Willen's brothers turned up missin', people thought ol' Riall musta done 'em. He didn't deny it. Acted like he didn't care whether he lived or died."

"What happened?"

"They had a trial, found Riall guilty." He leaned forward, squinting at her. "Catherine . . . is that you?"

She nodded, struggling for control. "What did they do with him?"

"How can it be you?" he said.   "Where you been?"

"What happened to my father?"

"God, Catherine.   You know what happens to them that's found guilty of murder. If it's any comfort, the truth come out finally."

"They took him in under the wing . . . they left him under the wing?"   Her fists clenched, nails pricking hard into her palm. "Is that what they did?"

He lowered his eyes, picked at a fray on his trouserleg.

Her eyes filled, and she turned away, facing the mossy overhang of the fronto-parietal plate. "You said the truth came out."

"That's right. A girl confessed to having seen the whole thing. Said the Willens chased you into Griaule's mouth. She woulda come forward sooner, but ol' man Willen had her feared for her life. Said he'd kill her if she told. You probably remember her. Friend of yours, if I recall. Brianne."

She whirled around, repeated the name with venom.

"Wasn't she your friend?" Weedlon asked.

"What happened to her?"

"Why . . . nothing," said Weedlon. "She's married, got hitched to Zev Mallison. Got herself a batch of children. I 'spect she's home now if you wanna see her. You know the Mallison place, don'tcha?"

"Yes."

"You want to know more about it, you oughta drop by there and talk to Brianne."

"I guess . . . I will, I'll do that."

"Now tell us where you been, Catherine. Ten years! Musta been something important to keep you from home for so long."

Coldness was spreading through her, turning her to ice. "I was thinking, Tim . . . I was thinking I might like to do some scaling while I'm here. Just for old time's sake, you know." She could hear the shakiness in her voice and tried to smooth it out; she forced a smile. "I wonder if I could borrow some hooks."

"Hooks?" He scratched his head, still regarding her with confusion. "Sure, I suppose you can. But aren't you going to tell us where you've been? We thought you were dead."

"I will, I promise. Before I leave . . . I'll come back and tell you all about it. All right?"

"Well, all right." He heaved up from his chair. "But it's a cruel thing you're doing, Catherine."

"No crueller than what's been done to me," she said distractedly. "Not half so cruel."

"Pardon," said Tim. "How's that?"

"What?"

He gave her a searching look and said,

"I was telling you it was a cruel thing, keeping an old man in suspense about where you've been. Why you're going to make the choicest bit of gossip we've had in years. And you came back with . . . "

"Oh! I'm sorry," she said. "I was thinking about something else."

The Mallison place was among the larger shanties in Hangtown, half-a-dozen rooms, most of which had been added on over the years since Catherine had left; but its size was no evidence of wealth or status, only of a more expansive poverty. Next to the steps leading to a badly hung door was a litter of bones and mango skins and other garbage. Fruit flies hovered above a watermelon rind; a gray dog with its ribs showing slunk off around the corner, and there was a stink of fried onions and boiled greens. From inside came the squalling of a child. The shanty looked false to Catherine, an unassuming facade behind which lay a monstrous reality — the woman who had betrayed her, killed her father — and yet its drabness was sufficient to disarm her anger somewhat. But as she mounted the steps there was a thud as of something heavy falling, and a woman shouted. The voice was harsh, deeper than Catherine remembered, but she knew it must belong to Brianne, and that restored her vengeful mood. She knocked on the door with one of Tim Weedlon's scaling hooks, and a second later it was flung open and she was confronted by an olive-skinned woman in torn gray skirts — almost the same color as the weathered boards, as if she were the quintessential product of the environment — and gray streaks in her dark brown hair. She looked Catherine up and down, her face hard with displeasure, and said, "What do you want?"

It was Brianne, but Brianne warped, melted, disfigured as a waxwork might be disfigured by heat. Her waist gone, features thickened, cheeks sagging into jowls. Shock washed away Catherine's anger, and shock, too, materialized in Brianne's face. "No," she said, giving the word an abstracted value, as if denying an inconsequential accusation; then she shouted it: "No!" She slammed the door, and Catherine pounded on it, crying, "Damn you! Brianne!"

The child screamed, but Brianne made

no reply.

Enraged, Catherine swung the hook at the door; the point sank deep into the wood, and when she tried to pull it out, one of the boards came partially loose; she pried at it, managed to rip it away, the nails coming free with a shriek of tortured metal. Through the gap she saw Brianne cowering against the rear wall of a dilapidated room, her arms around a little boy in shorts. Using the hook as a lever, she pulled loose another board, reached in and undid the latch. Brianne pushed the child behind her and grabbed a broom as Catherine stepped inside.

"Get out of here!" she said, holding the broom like a spear.

The gray poverty of the shanty made Catherine feel huge in her anger, too bright for the place, like a sun shining in a cave, and although her attention was fixed on Brianne, the peripheral details of the room imprinted themselves on her: the wood stove upon which a covered pot was steaming; an overturned wooden chair with a hole in the seat; cobwebs spanning the corners, rat turds along the wall; a rickety table set with cracked dishes and dust thick as fur beneath it. These things didn't arouse her pity or mute her anger; instead, they seemed extensions of Brianne, new targets for hatred. She moved closer, and Brianne jabbed the broom at her. "Go away," she said weakly. "Please . . . leave us alone!"

Catherine swung the hook, snagging the twine that bound the broom straws and knocking it from Brianne's hands. Brianne retreated to the corner where the wood stove stood, hauling the child along. She held up her hand to ward off another blow and said, "Don't hurt us."

"Why not? Because you've got children, because you've had an unhappy life?" Catherine spat at Brianne. "You killed my father!"

"I was afraid! Key's father . . . "

"I don't care," said Catherine coldly. "I don't care why you did it. I don't care how good your reasons were for betraying me in the first place."

"That's right! You never cared about anything!" Brianne clawed at her breast. "You killed my heart! You didn't care about Glynn, you just wanted him because he wasn't yours!"

It took Catherine a few seconds to dredge that name up from memory, to connect it with Brianne's old lover and recall that it was her callousness and self-absorption that had set the events of the past years in motion. But although this roused her guilt, it did not abolish her anger. She couldn't equate Brianne's crimes with her excesses. Still, she was confused about what to do, uncomfortable now with the very concept of justice, and she wondered if she should leave, just throw down the hook and leave vengeance to whatever ordering principle governed the fates in Hangtown. Then Brianne shifted her feet, made a noise in her throat, and Catherine felt rage boiling up inside her.

"Don't throw that up to me," she said with flat menace. "Nothing I've done to you merited what you did to me. You don't even know what you did!"

She raised the hook, and Brianne shrank back into the corner. The child twisted its head to look at Catherine, fixing her with brimming eyes, and she held back.

"Send the child away," she told Brianne.

Brianne leaned down to the child. "Go to your father," she said.

"No, wait," said Catherine, fearing that

the child might bring Zev Mallison.

"Must you kill us both?" said Brianne, her voice hoarse with emotion. Hearing this, the child once more began to cry.

"Stop it," Catherine said to him, and when he continued to cry, she shouted it.

Brianne muffled the child's wails in her skirts. "Go ahead!" she said, her face twisted with fear. "Just do it!" She broke down into sobs, ducked her head and waited for the blow. Catherine stepped close to Brianne, yanked her head back by the hair, exposing her throat, and set the point of the hook against the big vein there. Brianne's eyes rolled down, trying to see the hook; her breath came in gaspy shrieks, and the child, caught between the two women, squirmed and wailed. Catherine's hand was trembling, and that slight motion pricked Brianne's skin, drawing a bead of blood. She stiffened, her eyelids fluttered down, her mouth fell open — an expression, at least so it seemed to Catherine, of ecstatic expectation. Catherine studied the face, feeling as if her emotions were being purified, drawn into a fine wire; she had an almost aesthetic appreciation of the stillness gathering around her, the hard poise of Brianne's musculature, the sensitive pulse in the throat that transmitted its frail rhythm along the hook, and she restrained herself from pressing the point deeper, wanting to prolong Brianne's suffering.

But then the hook grew heavy in Catherine's hands, and she understood that the moment had passed, that her need for vengeance had lost the immediacy and thrust of passion. She imagined herself skewering Brianne, and then imagined dragging her out to confront a village tribunal, forcing her to confess her lies, having her sentenced to be tied up and left for whatever creatures foraged beneath Griaule's wing. But while it provided her a measure of satisfaction to picture Brianne dead or dying, she saw now that anticipation was the peak of vengeance, that carrying out the necessary actions would only harm her. It frustrated her that all these years and the deaths would have no resolution, and she thought that she must have changed more than she had assumed to put aside vengeance so easily; this caused her to wonder again about the nature of the change, to question whether she was truly herself or merely an arcane likeness. But then she realized that the change had been her resolution, and that vengeance was an artifact of her old life, nothing more, and that her new life, whatever its secret character, must find other concerns to fuel it apart from old griefs and unworthy passions. This struck her with the force of a revelation, and she let out a long sighing breath that seemed to carry away with it all the sad vibrations of the past, all the residues of hates and loves, and she could finally believe that she was no longer the dragon's prisoner. She felt new in her whole being, subject to new compulsions, as alive as tears, as strong as wheat, far too strong and alive for this pallid environment, and she could hardly recall now why she had come.

She looked at Brianne and her son, feeling only the ghost of hatred, seeing them not as objects of pity or wrath, but as unfamiliar, irrelevant, lives trapped in the prison of their own self-regard, and without a word she turned and walked to the steps, slamming the hook deep into the boards of the wall, a gesture of fierce resignation, the closing of a door opening onto anger and the opening of one that led to uncharted climes, and went down out of the village, leaving old Tim Weedlon's thirst for gossip unquenched, passing along Griaule's back, pushing through thickets and fording streams, and not noticing for quite some time that she had crossed onto another hill and left the dragon far behind. Three weeks later she came to Cabrecavela, a small town at the opposite end of the Carbonales Valley, and there, using the gems provided her by Mauldry, she bought a house and settled in and began to write about Griaule, creating not a personal memoir but a reference work containing an afterword dealing with certain metaphysical speculations, for she did not wish her adventures published, considering them banal by comparison to her primary subjects, the dragon's physiology and ecology. After the publication of her book, which she entitled *The Heart's Millenium*, she experienced a brief celebrity; but she shunned most of the opportunities for travel and lecture and lionization that came her way, and satisfied her desire to impart the knowledge she had gained by teaching in the local school and speaking privately with those scientists from Port

Chantay who came to interview her. Some of these visitors had been colleagues of John Colmacos, yet she never mentioned their relationship, believing that her memories of the man needed no modification; but perhaps this was a less than honest self-appraisal, perhaps she had not come to terms with that portion of her past, for in the spring five years after she had returned to the world she married one of these scientists, a man named Brian Ocoi, who in his calm demeanor and modest easiness of speech appeared cast from the same mold as Colmacos. From that point on little is known of her other than the fact that she bore two sons and confined her writing to a journal that has gone unpublished. However, it is said of her — as is said of all those who perform similar acts of faith in the shadows of other dragons yet unearthed from beneath their hills of ordinary-seeming earth and grass, believing that their bond serves through gentle constancy to enhance and not further delimit the boundaries of this prison world — from that day forward she lived happily ever after. Except for the dying at the end. And the heartbreak in between.